Enid Blyton

The Flyaway Money

...and other stories

Bounty
Books

Published in 2015 by Bounty Books,
a division of Octopus Publishing Group Ltd,
Carmelite House
50 Victoria Embankment,
London EC4Y 0DZ
www.octopusbooks.co.uk

An Hachette UK Company
www.hachette.co.uk
Enid Blyton ® Text copyright © 2011 Chorion Rights Ltd.
Illustrations copyright © 2015 Award Publications Ltd.
Layout copyright © 2015 Octopus Publishing Group Ltd.

Illustrated by Peter Wilks.

ISBN: 978-0-75373-063-8

A CIP catalogue record for this book is available from the
British Library.

Printed and bound by CPI Group (UK) Ltd, Croydon, CR0 4YY

CONTENTS

The
Flyaway Money

Willy sat indoors reading. It was a lovely day and the sun shone brightly out-of-doors. But Willy didn't go out.

The other children came by and called to him. "Come on, lazy. Come along out into the sun. It's lovely. You are an old stick-in-doors, you never come out with us for a walk."

"I don't like walking," said Willy.

"If you walked a bit more you wouldn't be so fat, and you'd get rosy cheeks like us," called Hannah. "Do come."

"I don't want to," said Willy. "I might go down to the village to spend some money my uncle has sent me. Look!"

He showed the banknote to the children. It was a lot of money.

"That's the only thing you go out for, except school!" shouted John. "To spend money! All you know about are the shops and the buses – you don't know anything about the golden buttercups in the fields, or the way the river shines, and I don't believe you've ever seen a baby rabbit!"

Willy frowned. He didn't like being teased. He was not a very healthy boy, as the others were, for he hardly ever went out into the woods and fields, he didn't like playing games, but just sat about lazily. He was fat and pale, and nobody really liked him very much.

"He reminds me of a slug or something," said Molly. "Poor Willy Slug – what a lot he misses!"

He did. He didn't see the first primroses in the wood. He didn't hear the merry song of the chaffinch in the hedges. He didn't hear the first cuckoo calling, and he didn't even find blackberries or nuts in the autumn.

The other children went on. Willy sat reading his book. His money lay on a table beside him. Suddenly the wind came in and blew it away! It blew the banknote right up into the air, and over the garden hedge!

"My money!" cried Willy, and jumped up. Out he went and chased his money. But the wind was in a playful mood that morning, and took away his money just as if it were playing a game.

Down the lane it blew it and into a field. Across the field it puffed it and over the stile. Into the woods flew the money, and Willy chased after it.

He couldn't see his money when he

got into the woods. They were very quiet and still. A bird was singing a little song to itself somewhere. Willy couldn't help listening.

"That's a nice little tune," he thought, and sat down to listen. He kept very quiet. Two rabbits suddenly popped out from behind a tree and began to play together.

"Oh!" thought Willy, in delight. "Look at that! Aren't they sweet?"

One rabbit suddenly sat up on its hind legs and began to wash itself. "Why, it really washes its face properly!" said Willy to himself in surprise. "It rubs its nose with its paws as if it had a sponge or flannel – and now it's bending its ears down to wash those."

The rabbits suddenly saw Willy, and they ran to their holes and disappeared. The bird stopped singing. Willy got up and went on through the wood, looking for his money.

He walked through the little wood and out at the other side. In front of him was a great sheet of shining gold.

"What can it be!"

Willy said in amazement. "Goodness

The Flyaway Money

me, it's thousands and thousands of buttercups!"

So it was. It was a good buttercup year, and the golden flowers waved in their thousands. They were beautiful. Each cup shone as if someone had polished it.

Willy picked some and looked at them. "They are like gold inside," he said. "I'll take some home to Mum. And some of this pink clover too – how pretty it is!"

The sun shone down and warmed him. The sky was as blue as the speedwells that winked blue eyes at him on the banks of the field. A big hare suddenly got up from the middle of the field and raced away as swift as lightning.

"This is a most exciting walk," said Willy to himself. "Why, there is the river!"

So it was, a blue shining river that was full of sparkles and ripples. "I'll walk along it and watch it," said Willy. "Oh – there goes a moorhen – and look at that family of ducks! One drake, one duck, and seven little yellow ducklings! How funny they are, all sailing along in a row."

He watched the ducks turn themselves upside down in the water to look for grubs

in the mud below. He wished he could do that too. If he learned to swim, perhaps he could.

Suddenly he heard someone shouting, "Hi, Willy, Willy! You said you didn't want to come out! You've walked a long way! How ever did you manage it?"

The other children were lying in the grass among the buttercups. They waved to Willy. He went over to them.

"I say – look at old Willy! Doesn't he look different!" said Hannah. "He's got red cheeks for once!"

"Well, he's walked a long way," said John. "Whatever made you do that, Willy?"

"The wind blew my money away and I

came after it," said Willy. "I saw a lot of things – I saw a rabbit washing itself – and I heard a bird sing such a funny little song to itself – and I saw a family ofducks – and I say, aren't the buttercups lovely!"

The other children looked at him. This was a new Willy, a Willy who had his eyes

and ears open, and could see and hear the lovely things around.

"We're going for a picnic into the hills tomorrow," said John. "Would you like to come? It's a long way – but you can see the sea from the hills."

"Yes, I'll come," said Willy. "I expect I'll be a bit slow, because I'm too fat, and my legs aren't strong and used to walking like yours. But I'd like to come."

He went home with the others. He gave his mother the buttercups and clover and she was so pleased. He hadn't found his money, but somehow Willy didn't seem to mind.

"I found a lot of other things instead," he said. "Things that are much nicer than money, Mum. I'm glad the wind blew away my money because I had such a lovely time. My legs are tired, but I don't mind."

"Better to have tired legs than lazy ones!" said his mother. "What fun you are going to have now, Willy!"

He is, isn't he? Soon he will lose his fat and his pale cheeks and his lazy ways, and he will be able to go for long walks, and play games, and enjoy all the lovely things in the countryside. What a good thing the wind blew away his money that morning!

The Bit of
Barley Sugar

Once when Simon bit a stick of barley
sugar, a piece of it broke right off and fell
on the floor.

Simon knelt down to look for it. "If you
find the bit you've dropped, you must go
and wash it before you eat it," said his
mother. "It may be dirty."

But Simon couldn't find it, though he
looked everywhere. He soon gave it up
and didn't bother about it any more.

But one of the toys had seen where it
went! The wooden bear belonging to the
Noah's ark had seen it roll right over the
carpet and go down a little mouse-hole in
the wall. He stared and stared at the hole.

"Tonight I'll go and look in the hole
and see if I can get out the barley sugar,"
he thought. "I shan't tell anyone at all. It
shall be my barley sugar!"

So that night when he thought no one was looking he went to the mouse-hole.

He bent down by the hole and put in his head. The barley sugar was just inside! The bear was pleased. But he didn't want to get it out in case the others saw him and came to share it. So he stood with his head inside the hole and licked the barley sugar. It was lovely and sweet.

The bear licked until he had had enough. He thought he would back out and go and play. He would go and have

another lick when he felt like it. He wouldn't tell anyone at all about that lovely barley sugar!

He backed out and looked round. The clockwork mouse was nearby, looking at him in great astonishment. "Why did you stand so long with your head in the hole?" he asked the wooden bear. "You looked funny."

"Mind your own business," the bear said rudely and went away. The clockwork mouse stood and thought for a minute and then he went to the hole. He stuck his head inside too – and dear me, what was that nice sweet smell?

"Barley sugar! A bit of barley sugar! And that bear's been licking it all by himself, the greedy thing!" thought the mouse. "I'll pull it out."

But he couldn't. So he, too, stood and licked and licked till he felt sick. Then he backed out quickly, hoping the bear hadn't seen him. He backed straight into one of the toy soldiers.

"Look out!" said the toy soldier, almost falling over. "Do tell me, clockwork mouse – why have you stood so still with your nose in the mouse-hole for such a very long time? You looked most peculiar!"

"Mind your own business," said the clockwork mouse, just as rudely as the bear, and ran away. The toy soldier was puzzled. Was there someone down the hole to talk to?

He went and stuck his head inside – and he saw the barley sugar at once! He tried to get right into the hole to get it, but he couldn't because his toy gun stuck fast. So he just put his head in as far as he could and licked. He licked and licked.

"Delicious!" he said. "But I can't lick any more. My tongue is very tired."

He backed out of the hole and saw one of the little doll's-house dolls watching him in surprise.

"What are you doing down that hole?" she said. "You did look funny."

"Mind your own business!" said the toy soldier, very rudely indeed, and he pointed his gun at her. She squealed and hid behind the brick-box. As soon as the toy soldier had gone she ran up to the mouse-hole and peeped down.

"A bit of barley sugar! Oh! So that's

what he keeps down there!" said the doll's-house doll. "Well, I'll have it all for myself."

But she couldn't get it out – so she, too, had to put in her head and lick. Lickity-lick! How nice and sweet it was. She was sorry when she couldn't lick any more.

She backed out – and dear me, there was a big skittle watching her in astonishment. "What are you doing? What's down there?" he said.

"Mind your own business!" said the doll, rudely, and went to wash her sticky face.

The skittle poked his wooden head down. What! Barley sugar! He poked at it with his head – and, alas, he poked it so far down the hole that he couldn't even lick it. He was very sad indeed. He came out, and went to tell the other skittles.

While he was gone the Noah's ark bear came up. He thought he would have another little lick, so he stuck his head inside the hole. But what had happened? He simply couldn't reach the barley sugar! It was much too far down – and will you believe it, when he tried to wriggle after it, he got stuck so fast that he couldn't get out of the hole.

He roared and wriggled – and a little live mouse came running up the hole in surprise. She bumped into the barley sugar. "Oh! Are you shouting to tell me you've pushed a bit of barley sugar down my hole for me to eat?" she cried. "Thank you very, very much, bear!" And she picked it up in her mouth and ran off with it down her hole to her nest.

The farmer from the toy farm pulled the bear out of the hole. The bear was very angry. "The mouse took my bit of barley sugar. She took it!"

"It wasn't yours, it was mine," said the clockwork mouse.

"Ooooh, fibber! It was mine!" said the toy soldier.

"No, no – it belonged to me!" said the doll's-house doll.

"It should have been mine," the skittle

said sadly. "But I poked it too far down the hole!"

"Oh – so it was you who did that!" roared the angry bear, and he flew at the skittle and knocked him over. Mr Noah came up from the Noah's ark, very cross to see such behaviour.

"Stop that now," he said. "Bear, clockwork mouse, soldier, doll's-house doll and skittle, go into the ark at once. Greediness must be punished. I'm ashamed of you all!"

And will you believe it, he shut them all up in his ark the whole night long, and they were very sad indeed, left by themselves in the dark. As for the barley sugar, the mouse's children have a lick at it for a reward whenever they are good. It won't last much longer. It's almost gone!

The Story of Lucky

One day, when Mary and Jack were walking home from school, they saw a crowd of children watching something. They ran up to see what it was.

"Oh," said Jack, angrily, "look, Mary. Those three boys in the middle have got a young puppy, and they're teasing it. What a shame! The poor little thing is terribly frightened."

"Well, no one seems to be doing anything about it," said Mary, "so we must. Come on, Jack, we'll rescue it."

The two children pushed their way through the others, and faced the three boys.

"Don't be so cowardly," said Jack, bravely. "Leave the puppy alone. Give it to me and I'll take it home, if it doesn't belong to anyone. It's a shame to tease a little thing like that."

Mary caught hold of the puppy and held it tight. One of the boys pulled her hair, but she didn't care. Another boy tried to push Jack over, but he wasn't going to run away, not he!

Then some of the other children came round the puppy, and said, "Poor little

thing! Mary and Jack are quite right to rescue it. Run away, you naughty boys, or someone will catch you."

Then Mary and Jack took the puppy home, and told their mother all about it.

"May we keep it?" asked Jack. "No one owns it, Mum. What shall we call it?"

"Yes, you may keep it, if it doesn't belong to anybody," said their mother. "Call it Lucky, for really it was very lucky to be rescued by you."

So they called it Lucky. It loved Jack and Mary, and grew into a big, strong dog. They always took Lucky for walks with them, and he used to go rabbit-hunting and was very happy indeed.

One day the three of them went for a walk by the lake. Lucky tore off after a rabbit and left Mary and Jack alone. And then a dreadful thing happened. Mary was walking just at the edge of the lake when suddenly her foot slipped, and over she went, right into the deep blue water!

Jack was frightened. Mary couldn't swim, and neither could he. He couldn't reach her, for the bank was high above the water. No one was about. What was he to do? Mary would drown if he didn't do something! Then he suddenly thought of Lucky.

"Lucky!" he shouted. "Lucky! Lucky! Come here, quick, Lucky!"

Lucky bounded up, and immediately he saw poor Mary struggling in the water below. *Splash!* In he jumped and swam to her. He caught hold of her dress in his strong teeth and swam to the shore, dragging her after him. He found a place

where the bank was low, and Jack helped to drag Mary out. She was gasping and spluttering, but in a few minutes she was all right again.

"Oh, Lucky!" she said, hugging him hard. "You saved my life! Brave Lucky! Good Lucky!"

"Wuff!" said Lucky, and licked her face. Then they all ran home to Mother.

"He has paid you back for rescuing him when he was a puppy," said Mother. "Hurrah for good old Lucky!" and she gave him three chocolate biscuits for a treat!

The Quarrelsome Brownies

Snippy and Snappy were two brownies who lived next door to one another. They were bad-tempered fellows, always quarrelling, and yet they always did everything together if they possibly could.

"Let's go blackberrying today, Snippy," said Snappy one morning.

"Very well," said Snippy. "I shall make a blackberry pudding."

"Oh, a blackberry tart is much nicer," said Snappy.

"No, a pudding is better," said Snippy. "You get lots of juice in a pudding – but if you make an open tart of blackberries you don't get any juice."

They quarrelled all the way to the woods about puddings and tarts – and then they began to pick their blackberries. They each had a big basket. The blackberries were very ripe and black, and they were as sweet as could be. Both brownies soon had black mouths, for they ate as many as they put in their baskets!

"I've got enough," said Snippy. "I shall go home."

"No, wait for me," said Snappy. "I want some more."

Snippy put his basket down on the ground and wandered off to look for nuts. Snappy went on picking fast – and as he picked he came nearer and nearer to Snippy's basket. He didn't see it, for he had his back to it.

Snippy, coming back from his search for nuts, suddenly yelled to Snappy.

"Hi! Look where you're putting your big feet! You'll upset my basket!"

Snappy jumped in fright, and his foot went into Snippy's basket. It upset – and all the blackberries rolled on the ground!

"Oh, you careless, careless brownie!" shouted Snippy in a rage. "Look at that!"

"Well, pick them up then," said Snappy. "It was your own fault, shouting at me like that and making me jump.

How was I to know I'd jump right into your silly basket?"

"It isn't a silly basket!" roared Snippy. "It's better than yours. And how can I pick up my blackberries when they have rolled over an ants' nest and ants are nibbling them all?"

"They won't hurt you," said Snappy.

"You just give me some of your blackberries!" cried Snippy, and he ran at Snappy. But the brownie was too quick for him, and he tore off through the woods with his basket. Snippy stopped, out of breath. He knew he would never catch Snappy. He went back to his blackberries.

"Oh dear!" he groaned in dismay. "Now the wasps have found them too. I really daren't pick them up. I'd pick up handfuls of ants and wasps as well! They'll have to stay there! Bother Snappy! He'll have a fine blackberry tart – and I won't have my blackberry pudding after all!" Snippy picked up his empty basket and went slowly home. The more he thought about Snappy's blackberry tart the angrier he became.

"I've a good mind to creep into Snappy's kitchen and see if I can't take his blackberries!" thought Snippy. "He upset mine – so why shouldn't I have his?"

When he got home he poked his nose over the wall to see what Snappy was doing. He heard him banging about in the kitchen, so he knew it was no use going to get the blackberries then. He would wait till it was dark!

And what was Snappy doing? He was so afraid that Snippy might come to take away his blackberries that he was busy cooking them already! He had madesome lovely pastry, and had cooked the blackberries with plenty of sugar. He took the tart out of the oven – a beautiful

tart, big, delicious, and spread so thickly with blackberries that there was hardly any pastry to be seen!

"Aha!" said Snappy to himself. "There's a fine tart! Snippy is silly to say that a blackberry pudding is better than a tart. He's quite wrong. If he hadn't been so horrid to me I might give him a piece. But I shan't now!"

Snappy put the beautiful tart on the bottom shelf of the larder to cool. He thought he would have some for supper that night.

"But it would be nice to have some cream with it," said Snappy. "I'll just run out and ask Dame Cheese for a jug of cream."

So out he went, carrying his little lantern, for by now it was getting dark. Snippy heard the front door bang and he grinned. Now was the time to steal into Snappy's kitchen and take away his basket of blackberries! Snippy didn't guess that Snappy had made them into a tart already!

He climbed over the wall. He pushed up the window and slipped inside. It was quite dark in the kitchen, and as Snippy didn't care to light a candle, he had to feel about in the dark for the blackberries.

He felt on the table. Nothing there. He felt on the dresser. Nothing there either. He felt on the shelf. No, no blackberries there. They must be in the larder. He opened the larder door. He felt about the shelves. He couldn't find any basket on the bottom shelf – nor on the next shelf – nor on the next one. Snippy couldn't reach the highest one of all and he felt sure that Snappy must have put the blackberries there – no doubt about it!

"Well, I can get up there if I stand on

the bottom shelf," said Snippy, quite determined to get those blackberries! So he stood on the bottom shelf and felt eagerly on the highest one with his hand.

And just as he was doing that he heard the front door open! It was Snappy who had come back again! Oh dear, dear, dear! Snippy got such a shock that he slipped and fell. He sat down *bang* on the bottom shelf – and will you believe it, although he didn't know it, he had sat down right in the middle of that lovely, juicy, blackberry tart! He had really!

Snappy heard the bang in the larder. It frightened him.

"What a very large mouse that must be," he said, trembling. He lit his candle and went to look. And to his very great surprise he saw Snippy in his larder, looking very much ashamed of himself!

"Snippy! Have you come to steal my tart?" cried Snappy. He flashed his candle round the larder. "Oh, you have, you have! It's gone! Have you eaten it?"

"I haven't taken your tart," said Snippy. "And I haven't even tasted it. I came for your blackberries. You spoilt mine, so I

37

thought you ought to give me yours."

"Where is my tart, my beautiful black-berry tart?" cried Snappy, in despair. "Even the dish has gone!"

Now you can guess where the black-berry tart was – sticking tightly to Snippy's trousers! So was the dish – but Snippy didn't know it.

"I'll help you look for the tart," he said to Snappy. But no matter where the two of them looked they could see no sign of that blackberry tart! Snippy sat down on a chair at last, and looked quite startled to hear the clang that the enamel dish made as he sat down.

Suddenly Snappy gave a shriek.

"Look! Look! Snippy, you are dripping ink all over the place! Oh, my nice carpet! Is your fountain pen leaking?"

Snippy took it out of his pocket to see. No, his pen was quite all right. He looked down at the black drops all over the carpet in amazement. How could he be leaking ink?

And then he felt behind himself – and he found the dish of blackberry tart there, sticking tightly to his trousers, dripping rich black juice everywhere!

"Snappy," said Snippy in a small voice, "I know where your blackberry tart is."

"Where?" said Snappy, looking all round.

"I'm sitting on it," said Snippy. "I must have fallen right into it in the larder, and didn't know."

He got up and turned himself round – and Snappy saw his blackberry tart there.

He looked as black as thunder at first – and then his mouth tilted upwards and he began to laugh – and laugh and laugh!

"Oh, Snippy, you do look so funny!" he said. "And dear me, how strange – I trod on your blackberries by mistake – and now you've sat on mine! We are even, Snippy, so let's stop quarrelling and go blackberrying again tomorrow."

"What about my lovely new trousers?" wailed Snippy, trying to wipe the tart off. "They are quite, quite spoilt."

"Well, you shouldn't have come sneaking into my larder," said Snappy, "I really think that serves you right."

"You horrid, mean, unkind thing!" cried Snippy; and in another moment both the quarrelsome little brownies were squabbling as hard as could be. They picked up bits of the blackberry tart and threw them hard at one another. *Squish! Squish!* What a mess there was!

It took Snappy a whole morning to clean up his kitchen the next day; and it took Snippy the whole morning to wash his nice new trousers.

They went off to find some more

blackberries in the afternoon – but whether they will manage to make puddings and tarts of them this time, I don't know! What do you think?

The
Dawdlers

"I never knew such a couple of dawdlers!" Mother said crossly. "Never in my life. Jane! Jack! Aren't you ready yet?"

The twins came up. "I was just looking at a book," said Jane.

"And I was only putting my train away," said Jack.

"It took you ten minutes to do that!" said their mother. "And now we shall have to run all the way to the station to catch the train. What dawdlers you are!"

Jane and Jack were going to their grandmother's. They were to stay with her for three days. How lovely! She had a lovely house and garden. There was a pond with goldfish, and a dog and a kitten to play with.

"Now don't you dawdle about when you stay with Granny," said Mother. "She's not as patient as I am. You must go when you are called, and you mustn't dawdle about and waste time."

"We won't," said Jane, and she really meant it. It would be such fun to stay with Granny! She had a tin of chocolate biscuits that stood on the mantelpiece, and was always ready for them when they went to see her. She had a way of giving unexpected treats, like going off to the zoo. She loved picnics, and she liked taking children to the little swimming pool not far away. You never knew what was going to happen at Granny's!

Their mother left them both there. Granny was very pleased to see them and

gave them each a hug. "I've made lots of little plans for you," she said. "Quite a programme in fact. And the children from next door are going to join in as well. We shall have some fun."

Everything went well till teatime. The two children were out playing with the puppy in the garden. Granny rang the tea bell and they finished their game. Then, hot and dirty, they dawdled indoors to wash their hands and tidy up.

Jane ran both taps to see how quickly she could fill the basin. Then Jack did it to see if he could fill it more quickly. Then they wiped their hands and took a very, very long time.

"Why were you so long?" asked Granny, when they came into the sitting-room. "I've almost finished. Mummy told me you were dawdlers, but you mustn't dawdle when you are visiting someone. I don't like it."

"Sorry, Granny," said the twins. They had to gobble down a perfectly lovely tea because Granny wanted to go out and see a friend and was taking the twins with her. What a waste of lovely cakes!

But, you know, it's very hard to break a bad habit, and the next day the twins were dawdling again! "I'll ring the bell for you to come in at eleven o'clock and have some chocolate biscuits and lemonade," said Granny. "Come straight in and don't dawdle."

The bell rang at eleven. Jane was lying down watching the goldfish in the pond. Jack was reading a book. Jane didn't stir when the bell went, and Jack finished his chapter. Then they dawdled indoors, smelling the flowers as they went.

And when they went indoors, what a shock! Granny was just going out shopping. The tin of biscuits was up on

45

the mantelpiece. There was no lemonade to be seen!

"You can't have biscuits and lemonade now," said Granny. "It's half past eleven, look – much too near your lunch-time. Go out and play again. And mind you don't find your lunch cleared away – you will if you dawdle!"

Well, that was a shock! No biscuits and no lovely sweet lemonade! They made up their minds to be in good time for lunch – and they were!

"Ah – no dawdling this time, I see," said Granny, ladling out some home-made soup. "It would have been a pity if you had missed your favourite soup! Now, listen. I've a real treat this afternoon. We're going to the zoo!"

"Ooooh!" said the twins together. "Really, Granny?"

"Yes, really," said Granny, smiling at them. "And the three children next door are going as well – and I've asked the little boy across the road. There's a coach stopping at our corner to pick us up. You can change into clean things, and be ready by half past two, sharp."

"We'll go and read on our beds till it's time to change," said Jane, thrilled at the thought of such a treat. So up they both went after lunch, and lay on their beds reading mystery stories.

"Time to change," said Jane at last. "Come on, Jack."

Jack didn't stir. He wanted to finish his story. Jane got ready. Then she found some old hats in the bottom drawer of her chest, and began to try them on.

"Oh, I do look funny!" she said, and tried on another. Then she dawdled about trying to find her clean socks. Jack was still reading.

A voice came up the stairs. "Are you ready? I'm just going to collect the other children."

It was Granny! Then the front door slammed, and Jane and Jack heard Granny's footsteps walking down the path.

"Gracious! It's nearly half past two!" said Jack, leaping off the bed. "Why didn't you tell me, Jane?"

Well, of course, when you are in a great hurry you simply can't find anything. Jane couldn't find her socks, Jack couldn't find his shoes. By the time they were ready, it was twenty to three. They raced out of the house to the corner – and far away in the distance they saw the coach rumbling along, taking Granny and the others to the zoo!

"They might have waited!" said Jane, and burst into tears.

"They waited for five minutes," said a gardener on a nearby lawn. "The driver

wouldn't wait after that."

The twins went back miserably to Granny's house. They found it locked up! The cleaning lady had thought they had gone with Granny, and had locked up and gone home. So there were the twins, locked out of the house for the whole afternoon – and no tea to be had either.

It was a miserable afternoon. Jane and Jack thought of elephants, feeding monkeys, watching lions and bears, and seeing the sea lions catching fish. What a lot they had missed!

"And all because we dawdled," said Jane. "How silly we are! We missed our biscuits and lemonade this morning, and our treat this afternoon – and we're missing our tea, too. I'm awfully hungry."

Granny came back that evening. The twins heard the other children thanking her for a wonderful treat. They went to meet her, not quite knowing what to say.

"Well, twins?" she said. "What happened to you? Didn't you want to go to the zoo? We waited five minutes for you and then the driver wouldn't wait any more. He said that either he must go on with us, or we must get out – and, of course, I couldn't disappoint the other children, could I?"

"No, Granny," said Jane. "I don't know how it happened that we were so late."

"Oh, I know," said Granny. "You just dawdled, didn't you? Well, dawdlers don't really need to be punished. They always punish themselves by losing lots of nice things through being slow. So I shan't punish you. I'll let you just punish yourselves while you're staying with me!"

But the twins didn't punish themselves again while they were with Granny! Oh, no! Not being able to go to the zoo had given them a tremendous shock. They were on time to go for a picnic the next day. They were ready before anyone else when Granny said she would take everyone swimming. They didn't miss

their chocolate biscuits and lemonade any more.

And now I've asked them to come to tea with me at four o'clock sharp. It's one minute to four – will they be on time? Yes – I can hear them coming. I shan't be able to call them dawdlers any more!

Who Would Have Thought It?

Farmer Gray was a horrid man. He had a bad temper, he was mean and nobody trusted or liked him. He got worse and worse, and at last no one would work for him. Then what a time he and his poor wife had, with the animals to feed, the stables and cowsheds to clean and any amount of other farm jobs to do!

Now one spring a little robin flew into the stable to hunt for a place to make a nest. She flew to a manger – no, that would be dangerous, for her nest might be eaten if she put it there. She flew to an old tin. Yes – that was good – but suppose it got thrown away?

She hunted all around and at last she found a very nice place. At least, she thought it was. She whistled to her little mate to come and see it. He flew into the stable.

"Look," carolled the hen-robin. "Here is a place for our nest – warm, cosy, the right size and a place not likely to be seen by anyone."

Where do you suppose this place was? In the pocket of Farmer Gray's old brown coat that he had hung up on the wall and forgotten! Well, who would have thought it? The cock-robin looked at the open pocket with bright black eyes.

"Yes," he said to his mate, "it's just the place for us. That pocket will hold all the grass roots, the leaves and the moss we use, and in this dark stable we shall be safe from weasels, stoats and jackdaws."

So they began to build their nest in the pocket of the farmer's old coat. They made a fine nest. They wove thin grass roots together, they tucked up the holes with moss and dead leaves, and they found plenty of soft hen feathers from the farmyard to line the nest softly.

They were very proud of it indeed. Robins always love to nest in anything belonging to humans – and this was a fine place. Soon the hen-robin laid four pretty

eggs with red-brown markings. She sat on them day after day. Sometimes the cock took a turn too, so that the hen-robin might stretch her wings. He brought her many tit-bits and sometimes sang a little creamy song to her. They took no notice of the horses stamping in the stable. They got used to the hens coming in and clucking loudly. They were happy and peaceful, looking forward to the hatching of their pretty eggs.

Now one day Farmer Gray got his coat soaking wet in a rainstorm. He took it to his wife and asked her to dry it.

"Oh dear!" she said. "What are you going to wear now? Your other coat is wet too. What's become of that old brown coat you used to have?"

Farmer Gray frowned. What had he done with it? Ah – he remembered. It was in the stable, of course – it had been hanging there for months!

"It's in the stable," he said. "I'll fetch it."

Off he went. He came to the stable and looked round. "Now where's that coat of mine?" he said.

The hen-robin was sitting on her eggs in the pocket and she heard him. Her small heart beat fast in fright. Oh surely, surely Farmer Gray did not want his old coat

now – just when her eggs were due to hatch at any minute! Oh no, no!

The cock-robin was perched nearby. He ruffled up his feathers in fear. What! Take the coat, and crush the nest and break the eggs? Oh no, Farmer Gray! You are a cross, rough man, and nobody likes you – but don't, don't do that!

Farmer Gray saw his coat. "Good! There it is," he said, and went over to it. The cock-robin gave a loud warble and the farmer looked round in surprise. What was the robin singing at him for? And then he suddenly knew the answer.

He saw the nest in the pocket of his coat as it hung on the nail. Dead leaves and bits of moss hung out of it. A small hen-robin, her red breast showing up clearly, sat in the pocket on the nest, her anxious black eyes looking trustfully at Farmer Gray.

The farmer looked down at her. He frowned and put out his hand to take the coat. And then he looked into the robin's

trustful eyes, and remembered something. He remembered how, when he had been a little boy, a robin had nested in an old boot of his father's, and how delighted he had been and how sweet the baby robins had looked about the garden. He stood and thought for a minute or two.

"Ah well, you can have my coat," he said to the little robins. "Maybe you need it more than I do!" And with that he went out into the yard without a coat on.

The robins sang for joy. Farmer Gray heard them, and for the first time for years his heart was warm. It was good to be kind to another creature, even if that creature was only a robin. He saw a man going by and he called him. "Hi, John! Come and see here for a minute!" The man came up in surprise, for it was seldom that Farmer Gray spoke nicely to anyone. The farmer took him to see the robins' nest in his old coat pocket.

"That'll bring you luck, William," said John.

"I need some," said Farmer Gray. "Here's spring come along and I've no one to help me with the farm."

John looked at Farmer Gray and
he thought, "Well, here's a man that
everyone hates – and yet he's let the
robins have his coat. He can't be so bad
after all. I've a good mind to come and
help him a bit."

"Well, William," he said out loud, "I'll
come and give you a hand when I've
finished at Farmer Brown's over the hill."

Farmer Gray was pleased. He went
to the farm and told his wife about the
robins and about how John was going to
work for him.

"Those robins will bring me luck," he
said, and he laughed. His wife was glad.
She had been lonely without any friends
to speak to.

John came. He worked hard. He got
another man to come. Everything went
well. The robins hatched out their eggs,
and baby robins fluttered in the old stable.
Farmer Gray brought them meal-worms
and they grew so tame that they would fly
on to his shoulders. How proud Farmer
Gray was then! He called all sorts of
people in to see his tame robins – and
that meant giving them something to eat

and drink. Soon the farmer had plenty of friends, and he forgot to frown and grumble.

"Here, my dear. Here's money to buy you a new dress and a new hat," said Farmer Gray to his wife. "We're making money. Things are better. We've got friends to help us. My word! Those robins have brought me luck all right."

"It wasn't really the robins," said his

wife. "It was the bit of kindness in your heart, William, that made you spare the robins and their nest. If you had not had that bit of kindness, you would have had no good luck!"

And she was right, wasn't she? We make our own good luck, there's no doubt about that!

The Boy Who
Scribbled

Bobby was an awful nuisance wherever he went, because he scribbled over everything! He always took his pencils and crayons with him – and, dear me, how he scribbled on walls, seats, and pavements!

"Bobby, it is very bad manners to scribble over things like that," said his mother.

"Bobby, you've spoilt our nice new garden seat by scribbling your name all over it," his aunt said crossly.

"Bobby, if you scribble on your desk again, you will stay in after school and write out 'I must not scribble' one hundred times," said his teacher.

But Bobby went on scribbling. You may have seen some of his scribbles, for he scribbled everywhere. Sometimes he wrote horrid things. Once, when Ellen wouldn't lend him her book, he wrote "Ellen is a selfish girl" all over her wall in white chalk. Her mother was very angry.

The policeman was angry too, because Bobby's town tried to keep the streets clean and tidy, there were litter bins everywhere and nobody was supposed to make a mess on the walls or fences. But Bobby simply couldn't help it.

His mother took away his crayons and his pencils. But Bobby found a sharp white stone and wrote all over the pavement with it. He was cross with George, so he wrote "George is a horrid boy" three times. George was very angry when he saw it.

Now, one day Bobby went for a picnic in a wood all by himself. He had a basket packed with goodies, and he meant to have a good time. He found a little path he hadn't seen before, and off he went into the very heart of the wood. And when he came there he found a pretty little whitewashed house, with a neat whitewashed wall round it, and bright flowers growing in the garden!

Bobby was astonished. He stared at the

house in surprise. "I didn't know anyone lived in this wood," he said to himself. "What a dear little house! I think I'll have my picnic here, and then I can go and ask for a drink of water at the house if I'm thirsty."

So he sat down nearby and undid his basket of food. There were sandwiches, cake, and apples, with a bar of chocolate to finish the meal. Bobby enjoyed it very much.

"Now for a drink!" he said. He got up and went to the little white gate. He opened it, went up the neat path, and knocked at the little white door.

But nobody came. Nobody seemed to be in the house at all. "Bother!" said Bobby. "Just when I wanted a drink!"

He went round the back to see if anyone was there. The dustbin was there, and the coal bunker. A piece of coal lay on the ground. Bobby picked it up.

And then you can guess what that naughty little boy did! He began to scribble over the white walls of the cottage with the coal. He drew some little men. He drew a house with chimneys. He wrote his own name again and again – Robert William Tomkins, Robert William Tomkins.

The coal made very black lines which showed up well on the house. When Bobby had finished scribbling on the white walls, he began to scribble on the walls of the garden. He wrote "This is a silly house. There is no one to give me a

drink". What a thing to do!

Then he wrote two or three things
about his school friends. He put "Harry
has carroty hair. Jane has rabbit-teeth.
John is a crybaby."

Just as he was finishing this, he heard
a noise. He looked up and saw six little
pixie men coming through the wood.
They hadn't seen him because he was
sitting beside the garden wall.

Bobby felt frightened. Six little men!
They might be very angry with him for
scribbling. He looked at the house – yes,
he had done a dreadful lot of scribbles

there. The naughty little boy quietly picked up his basket and, bending down to hide himself behind the wall, ran off into the wood without being seen.

When the six little men came up to their house they stared in horror at their white walls, which were now all spoilt with the black coal marks.

"Who has done this shocking thing?" said the chief little man in anger.

"Just look!" cried another. "All the way round our lovely house! Some horrid nuisance of a scribbler has been here."

"If only we knew who it was!" said the

chief man. "I would punish him well!"

"I can tell you who he is," said the third little man, and he pointed to where Bobby had written his name again and again – Robert William Tomkins, Robert William Tomkins. "Look, that's his name!"

"Ha!" said the chief man, looking stern. "So that's who he is. I've heard of him before. Well, he'll be sorry for this!"

"Yes," said the little men, going to get cloths and water to wash their walls. "Yes – he'll be sorry for this!"

The little men soon found out where Bobby lived. And then one of them stayed near Bobby all day long, although the boy didn't know it. The little men watched all he did. They saw him smack Nora. They saw him throw a stone at a cat. They heard him being rude to old Mrs Lucy. Oh, they soon found out quite a lot about Bobby!

And then strange things began to happen. One day when Bobby and his mother came home from a walk, they found their green front door painted all over with big red letters. And this is what was written on the door – BOBBY IS A HORRID RUDE BOY.

"Good gracious!" said his mother. "Look at that! Whoever has written that on our front door? We must get it off at once."

But they couldn't get it off, because it was painted with magic paint! So there it was for everyone to read when they went by. Bobby was angry and ashamed. He remembered that he had been rude to old Mrs Lucy, and he was careful to be polite the next time in case she had written the message!

The next thing that happened was a long message, painted in bright green on the pavement outside Bobby's house: BOBBY IS VERY UNKIND AND SELFISH. HE HAS BIG EARS. HE IS UNKIND TO ANIMALS! HA HA!

"Oh dear!" said Bobby's mother, nearly in tears. "Who can have done that on our pavement? Bobby, how I wish you had never had that dreadful habit of scribbling over everything! Now you see what has happened! Other people are scribbling things about you too."

Bobby was red with shame. How

dreadful that everyone who came by should read those things about him! He went to look at his ears. Yes – they were big. Well, he had teased Harry about his red hair, so perhaps it was Harry who had painted the horrid message on the pavement, and had put that Bobby had big ears.

Harry said he hadn't done anything

of the sort. "I'm not a silly scribbler like you!" he cried. "All I can say is that it serves you right for being such a horrid scribbler yourself!"

The next day the nice red walls of the house were painted white with comical pictures of Bobby and his big ears. Bobby cried and cried, he was so ashamed. His mother and father went to the policeman about the scribbles, and begged for his help.

"Well, I don't feel much inclined to help that boy of yours," said the policeman. "I've had plenty of trouble from him over scribbling on walls and pavements, I can tell you. If you ask me, I think this just serves him right!"

But all the same the policeman kept an eye on Bobby's house that night – and when he saw six funny little men creeping up with pails and brushes, he walked up to them with a large frown.

"Now then, what's all this?" he began in a very deep voice – but to his great surprise every single one of the little men vanished! Yes, disappeared into thin air, and not even a paintbrush was left!

That was the end of the scribbling on Bobby's house. The little men came no more. Bobby's father had the house repainted, and the front door, too, and

sent someone to clean the pavement outside. Then he spoke sternly to Bobby.

"All this has happened because of your horrid scribbling habits," said Mr Tomkins. "Have you anything to say to me about them, Bobby?"

"I'll never scribble anywhere again, Daddy," said Bobby in a low voice. And since then he never has. I'd hate to have horrid things scribbled about me by those six little men, wouldn't you?

Oh, What
a Pity!

Tessie had a bicycle, and all the other boys and girls thought she was very lucky, because it really was a nice one.

At first she lent it to anyone who wanted to try and ride it, but when Harry had dented the mudguard and Jane had broken a pedal, Tessie's mother said she was not to lend it to any child except in her own garden.

Susan was cross when she heard this. "Oh, how mean of your mother!" she said. "She might let you lend it in the road, Tessie!"

"Mummy isn't mean," said Tessie, who would never let anyone say a word against her mother. "It's just that she paid a lot of money for my bike, and she doesn't want it spoilt. She's not mean."

"Well, you ask me to tea and then I

can ride your bike in the garden," said
Susan. So Tessie told her mother that
Susan wanted to come to tea so that she
could ride the bicycle.

"Susan always wants to push in and get
her own way," said Tessie's mother. "No,
I can't have her to tea just yet, Tessie.
You are having your cousin for the day
this week, and Harry is coming to tea on
Tuesday. You can't have Susan."

Susan was cross. "Well, I said it before
and I say it again – your mother is mean!"
she said to Tessie. Tessie walked off
without a word. She was not going to
quarrel with Susan, but she wasn't going
to stay with her if she said things like
that.

Susan soon tried to make Tessie friends
with her again, because she so badly
wanted to ride Tessie's bicycle. So she
gave her a sweet, and told her that she
was the nicest girl in the class. When
Tessie was sucking the sweet and was
nice and friendly once more, Susan asked
for a ride.

"Let me have a little ride, just a tiny
little ride on your bike," she said. "We'll

wait till all the other boys and girls have
gone, Tessie, then no one will see. I'll
ride it down the lane, that's all. Please
do let me."

"Mummy said I wasn't to," said Tessie.

"Well," said Susan, thinking of another
idea. "Well, Tessie, you just turn your
back for a minute – and I'll hop on the
bike and ride off without you seeing.
Then it won't matter, because, you see,
you won't have lent me the bike, I shall
have taken it. Please, please, do let me
have a ride, Tessie. You're so lucky to
have a bike."

"Well," said Tessie, hardly liking to say no, because she saw how much Susan wanted a ride. "Well – just this once, then."

She turned her back. Susan jumped on to the bike and rode away down the lane. How fast she rode! How grand she felt!

Just as she passed a field a cow came out of the gate, the first of a herd driven out by the farmer. Susan was so frightened that she wobbled and fell off. *Crash!* She fell on her side and grazed her arm badly, and tore her dress.

Tessie heard the crash and turned. She ran to Susan and helped her up. "Oh – I knew I shouldn't have let you ride my bike," she said. "I knew I shouldn't! Look at your poor arm – and what will your mother say about your torn dress?"

The bicycle was not damaged, which was lucky. Susan picked it up, brushed her dress down, and looked at her bleeding arm. "Bother!" she said. "That stupid cow! It made me fall off."

"Well, you shouldn't have been on the bike, should you, really?" said Tessie, taking it. "You shouldn't have told me to turn my head away so that you could take it without my seeing you. It's a good thing the bike isn't damaged. Mummy would have been cross with you – and with me, too, for disobeying her."

Susan went home, trying to hide her torn dress and grazed arm. But her mother saw them both at once.

"Susan! What have you done to your arm? Did you fall down? And how did you tear your dress?"

"I was riding Tessie's bike," said Susan, not liking to tell her mother a story. "A cow came out of a gate and scared me, and I fell off."

"Susan, you are not to ride other people's bicycles," said her mother, at once. "For two reasons – one is that you may damage someone else's bike, and the other is that you haven't had enough practice in riding, and until you have you are not to ride in the road. You might have a bad accident."

"I wouldn't," said Susan, looking sulky.

"Now, do you understand, Susan?" said her mother. "I mean it. You are not to ride Tessie's bicycle, or anyone else's. One day you will have one of your own, and then you can practise riding it round and round your own garden till you can ride well enough to go out into the road. Be patient and wait till then."

Susan didn't feel at all patient. How could she wait perhaps for years for a bicycle? She knew that a bicycle was expensive, and she knew that her mother hadn't a lot of money to spare. She might have to wait till she was twelve before she had a bicycle – and she wasn't even nine till next week! How she wished she could have a bicycle for her ninth birthday! That would be great.

Her arm soon healed. Her dress was mended. Once or twice her mother warned her to remember what she had said about Tessie's bicycle.

"You will remember that I don't want you to ride Tessie's bicycle again, won't you?" she said. "And I hear that Tessie's mother has asked her not to lend it to anyone, too – so on no account must you borrow it, Susan."

Susan didn't say anything. She meant to have another ride whenever she could!

Her mother noticed that she said nothing and spoke sharply.

"Susan! Will you promise me not to ride on Tessie's bicycle?" she said.

"All right," said Susan, sulkily. How tiresome to have to promise! "I wish I could have a bike for my birthday next week, Mummy! Tessie was only nine when she had hers."

"Bicycles are so expensive," said Susan's mother. "And you are not very old yet. There is plenty of time for you to have a bicycle, Susan!"

Susan didn't ask Tessie for a ride any more that week. She watched her riding to and from school very enviously, but she didn't beg for a turn, too. She didn't want to upset Tessie, or to break her own promise.

The next week came. The day before her birthday came, Susan told everyone it was her birthday the next day, and she felt excited because she knew her mother was making her a cake with nine candles on it, and she thought she was having a new dress too.

Now, as Susan went home from school

that afternoon, she suddenly saw Tessie's bicycle leaning against the wall that ran round Harry's garden in the main road! Yes, there it was, bright and shining. Tessie must have gone in to see Harry's white mice.

"The road's empty. I'll just jump on Tessie's bike and have a little ride!" thought Susan. "No one will know. I'll go round the corner and back."

Quite forgetting her promise, Susan jumped on the bicycle and rode down the

road. She went fast, pedalling up and down strongly. She rang the bell at the corner. *Ting-a-ling-a-ling!* It sounded really good.

Then she put the brakes on to see if they worked. But they didn't work very well. Tessie had been told that she must take her bicycle to the shop to have the brakes put right, or else she might have an accident.

"Now I'd better go back," thought Susan to herself, and turned to go back. She had pedalled up the hill, and now it would be fun to go down it without pedalling at all!

She simply flew down! It was quite a steep hill. Suddenly, round the corner, came a tractor pulling a heavy trailer behind it.

Susan wobbled. She rang her bell but the farmer took no notice. She put on the brakes to slow the bicycle down – but they didn't work! The bicycle flew on and on, and it seemed as if the big tractor blocked up the whole of the road.

Just before she reached the tractor, Susan tried to jump off the bike. But it was going too fast for her to jump properly. She slipped, the bicycle flew straight in front of the tractor, and Susan herself rolled over and over and over at the side of the road.

She sat up, gasping, looking at herself

to see if she was hurt. But she wasn't! There didn't seem even to be a bruise or a scratch.

Then she looked round for the bicycle. But oh, what a pity, it was completely ruined. One of the tractor's big wheels had run over it before the farmer could stop. The wheels were buckled and broken. The handlebars were twisted. The right pedal was off and the left one was bent.

"Oh! Look at Tessie's bike!" said Susan, with tears in her eyes. The farmer was trying to pull it from under the tractor. He thought the bicycle was Susan's.

"I'm afraid your bike's done for," he said. "Why did you ride so fast down the hill? That was very silly of you. I might have run you over."

Susan didn't know what to do. Crying bitterly, she dragged the poor broken bike home at last, and her mother came running out to see whatever was the matter.

"Oh, Mummy – oh, Mummy – look at Tessie's bike!" wept Susan. "I broke my promise. I took it when Tessie was at Harry's – and I fell off it and a tractor ran over it. Oh, Mummy, what shall I do?"

Her mother looked in horror at the bicycle. "Are you hurt?" she said to Susan. Susan shook her head. "Well, you might easily have been killed, Susan. And look at Tessie's bike! Whatever will her father and mother say?"

"I don't know, I don't know!" wailed Susan. "Oh, why did I disobey you and break my promise? Tell me what I'm to do!"

Susan's mother looked very grave. She

set the broken bicycle by the fence, and took Susan's arm. "Come with me," she said. "I will show you what you must do."

She took Susan to the shed, which was locked. She unlocked it. Inside was a brand-new, very beautiful, shining bicycle! Susan gave a gasp when she saw it.

"Look," said her mother. "Daddy and I bought this for your birthday tomorrow, for a big surprise. Now, Susan, I am afraid you must take it to Tessie instead, because you have completely spoiled her bicycle. Maybe we can get Tessie's mended for you – I don't know – but you will certainly have to give up your new bicycle to Tessie."

Oh, what a pity! Oh, what a terrible pity to have to give up such a beautiful bicycle to somebody else, all because of a moment's disobedience and a broken promise. How Susan cried! How she wept and wailed! But she knew her mother was right. It was the only thing to do.

So now Tessie has Susan's beautiful bicycle, and Susan is waiting to hear if Tessie's old one can be mended. Poor Susan – it was very hard for her, wasn't it, but, as her mother said, you never know what may happen if you are disobedient, or break a solemn promise!

The Little
Paper-Folk

One very wet afternoon Jimmy and Susan
thought they would cut out pictures
from a book. Mother said they might, so
they found their scissors, took two old
magazines from the newspaper box in the
garage, and went to the living-room to cut
out.

"I'm going to cut out these motor-cars,"
said Jimmy. "They're good ones, all in
colour. Look, Susan."

"Yes," said Susan. "Well, I shall cut out
some people. See, there's an old woman
carrying a basket, and a tall man in a top
hat, and a little man in a dressing-gown. I
shall cut out lots of people."

Jimmy soon cut out his cars. There were
three – one red, one green, and one blue.
Then he thought he would cut out smaller
things. There was a fish-slice, a kitchen

spoon, a ladle, and a whisk on one page, so he cut those out. Then he found a page of boxes of chocolates, all with their lids open to show the chocolates inside. They did look delicious.

"I shall cut out these boxes of chocolates," he said to Susan. "Oh, what a nice lot of little people you have cut out! Stand them up against something, Susan. They will look real then."

Susan stood them up. There was the old woman, the tall man, the little man in a dressing-gown, a green imp, and a fat boy bouncing a ball. She stood them all up against a book.

"We've cut out lots of things," she said,

"cars and people, kitchen tools, and boxes of chocolates. Oh, Jimmy, wouldn't it be lovely if those chocolates were real?"

"Let's take everything we've cut out to the big windowsill," said Jimmy, gathering up his paper cars and other things. "We'll stand the cars up and the people too. They will look splendid."

So they went to the windowsill, behind the big blue curtain, and began to stand up all their paper things.

"I wish, I wish we were as small as these little people," said Susan. "Then we could play with them and see what they are really like."

Well, I don't quite know how it happened, but there must have been some magic about that day, for no sooner had Susan wished her wish than it came true!

Yes, it really did! She and Jimmy grew smaller and smaller and they felt very much out of breath, for it all happened so quickly. But when at last they stopped growing small, they found themselves on the windowsill with the paper people and cars. And the paper people were alive!

They smiled at Susan and Jimmy, and

came to shake hands with them. Their hands were funny – all flat and papery – and when the old woman turned round

Jimmy saw that she hadn't a proper back – there were printed letters all over her!

"That's the other side of the page she was cut out of!" whispered Jimmy, as he saw Susan's look of surprise. "There was a story on the other side, and that's part of it. Isn't it strange?"

"We are glad you cut out such lovely boxes of chocolates for us," said the man in the top hat, picking up a box and looking at it.

"And I'm glad you cut out my ball for

me," said the little fat boy. He began to bounce the ball but, alas, it would not bounce properly, because Susan's scissors had cut into the ball in one little place.

The boy was cross. "The ball won't bounce properly," he said frowning. "You were careless when you cut it out! I don't like you after all!"

"Don't take any notice of him," said the little man in the dressing-gown. "He's a bad-natured boy. I am pleased with the way you cut out my dressing-gown. Look, even my belt is well cut out, so that I can tie it round me."

The man in the top hat picked up a box of chocolates and offered them to Susan.

But she couldn't get her fingers into the box! You see, it was only a painted box, so of course the chocolates couldn't be taken out. She was so disappointed.

"I can't take out any of the chocolates," she said, trying hard.

The green imp she had cut out came and looked at the box. He put up his little green hand, and, to Susan's surprise, he picked out a handful of the chocolates and ran off with them.

"I expect he can do it because he's made of paper like the chocolates," whispered Jimmy. "Anyway, they'd taste horrid, I'm sure!"

"Let's go for a ride in these cars," cried the old woman with the basket. They ran to the cars. The tall man took the wheel of the red car and the old lady climbed in beside him. That left the imp all alone with the green car, and he looked as black as thunder.

"I can't drive a car," he said. "One of you children must get in with me and drive me along. I'm not going to be left out!"

"I don't want to get in the car with you," said Jimmy. "I don't like the look of you."

"You nasty boy!" cried the imp, in a rage. "Get into the car at once. How dare you insult one of the paper-folk!"

To Jimmy's surprise all the other paper-folk sided with the green imp. They shouted angrily to the children:

"Get in and drive him! Get in and drive him! You wouldn't eat our chocolates, and now you're too grand to drive our car!"

The children felt quite scared. Jimmy went to the green car and tried to get in. But of course he couldn't because it was only paper. He tried and tried, but his leg simply slid down the paper to the ground.

The imp was sitting in the back, watching. He frowned at Jimmy, and cried out crossly, "You're only pretending not to be able to get in. You're only pretending! Why can't you get in? You're the same as us, aren't you, and we got in!"

"Well, we're not the same as you, so there!" said Jimmy, losing his temper. "You're only made of paper – you haven't even got proper backs! We're real. You're just cut-out people; and your cars are cut-out cars, so of course we can't get into them! Don't be so silly!"

Well, when the paper-folk heard Jimmy saying that, they were all as hurt and angry as could be. They climbed out of the cars and looked all round them for something to fight the children with. They suddenly saw the fish-slice, the ladle, the kitchen spoon, and the whisk that Jimmy had cut out, lying on the ground by the boxes of chocolates.

The tall man picked up the fish-slice, and the man in the dressing-gown picked up the kitchen spoon. The imp snatched up the ladle. The old woman used her basket and the boy took the whisk to fight with, and together all the paper-folk rushed angrily at the scared children.

"Don't be frightened, Susan," said

Jimmy. "They're only paper."

"But we haven't anything to fight them with," cried Susan, looking round on the windowsill.

"Let's blow them with our breath," shouted Jimmy. "They are only paper, you know."

So, much to the cut-out people's surprise, as soon as they were close to the children, Jimmy and Susan blew hard at them with all their breath.

"Wheeew!" went the children together,

and the paper-folk were all blown over flat! What a surprise for them! They picked themselves up and rushed at the children once more.

"Wheeeew!" blew Jimmy and Susan, and once again the paper-folk were blown down flat – and, oh my, the fat boy was blown right over the edge of the windowsill on to the floor below. How the paper-folk screamed to see him go!

"I shan't have much breath left soon," whispered Jimmy to Susan. "Whatever shall we do?"

"I wish we could grow to our own size again," wailed Susan, who had had quite enough of being small.

Well, she only had to wish for it to become true, for there was still a little magic floating about in the air. Just as the paper-folk were rushing at them again the children shot up tall, and the cut-out people cried out in surprise.

In an instant the children were their own size, and at that moment they heard their mother's voice.

"Wherever are you? Jimmy! Susan! I've been looking for you everywhere!"

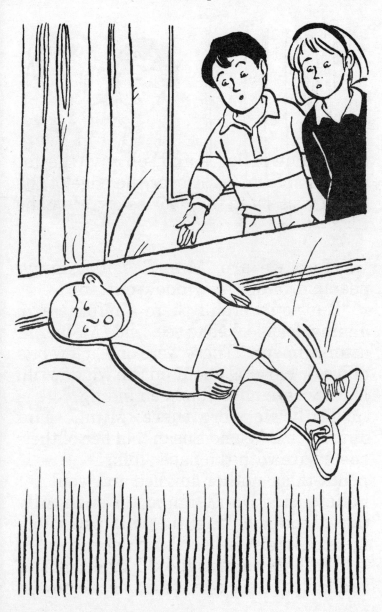

"Here we are, Mum," said Jimmy, peeping round the window-curtain.

"But you weren't there a minute ago, Jimmy, for I looked to see," said Mother in astonishment. "There were only a few bits of paper blowing about on the windowsill. Now, where have you been hiding?"

"Truly we were there, Mum," said Jimmy, and he and Susan told her of their adventure with the paper-folk.

But their mother laughed and wouldn't believe it. "Don't make up such silly tales," she said. "Fighting with paper-folk indeed! Whoever heard such nonsense?"

"Well, Mummy, look!" cried Susan suddenly. "Here's that nasty little boy on

Little Paper-Folk*

the floor, with his ball. Jimmy blew him over the edge of the windowsill. That just proves we are telling the truth."

It did, didn't it? The children and their mother looked at the paper boy on the floor, and at the other paper-folk who were all lying quietly on the windowsill.

"I should stick them firmly into your scrapbook," said Mother. "Then they won't do any more mischief!"

So that's where the paper-folk are now – in the middle of the scrapbook, glued down tightly. You can see them there any time you go to tea with Jimmy and Susan!

Jimmy and
the Jackdaw

Once there was a boy called Jimmy. When he had a birthday his uncle gave him a book all about birds.

There were pictures of birds in it and pictures of birds' eggs too.

"Aren't they pretty?" Jimmy said to his friend Connie. "Look at this picture of hedge-sparrows' eggs – they are as blue as the sky. I've a good mind to look for a hedge-sparrow's nest and take the eggs for myself."

"Oh, you mustn't do that," said Connie at once. "It isn't kind to take the eggs out of a bird's nest. You know you mustn't do it."

Jimmy didn't listen. It was springtime, and many birds were building their nests. Jimmy saw them flying here and there with bits of straw or a feather in their beaks.

"I shall look out for a hedge-sparrow's nest and take the eggs," thought Jimmy. "I shall put the eggs into a box lined with cotton wool. No one will know."

Well, he did find a hedge-sparrow's nest. It was in the hawthorn hedge that ran beside the lane. Jimmy saw the bird fly into it, and he tiptoed to the hedge.

He parted the sprays and peeped into the heart of the hedge. At first he couldn't see the nest, and then suddenly he did. It was well tucked away, hidden by the green leaves.

And in the nest was the mother hedge-

sparrow, sitting on her eggs, keeping them warm! She looked at Jimmy, but she did not move.

"Fly away, fly away!" said Jimmy, and he shook the hedge. It was very unkind of him. The little brown bird was afraid. She flew up from her nest and perched on a nearby tree, watching anxiously.

Jimmy saw the pretty blue eggs there, four of them. He was so greedy that he took them all. He did not leave the little mother bird even one.

She was very unhappy. She flew back to her nest after Jimmy had gone and looked sadly into it. Where were her pretty, very precious eggs? They were gone. The little hedge-sparrow burst into a sad little song, and told the other birds around the dreadful thing that had so suddenly happened to her.

Jimmy went home with the eggs. They looked so very pretty on the white cotton wool in the box. They were so pretty that he thought he would like to draw and paint them. Jimmy was very, very good at drawing and painting.

"Now, where's my silver pencil?" said

Jimmy. "I can easily draw these eggs. I think I will draw a nest first and then draw the blue eggs inside."

Jimmy began to draw with his silver pencil. He was very proud of that pencil, because he had won it at school as a drawing prize. No other boy had a silver pencil. Jimmy felt important when he took it out of his pocket at school to use it.

The next nest he found was a robin's. It was built on the ground under a hedge in Jimmy's own garden. There were four

eggs in it, and Jimmy took them all. The robin made an angry clicking noise at him, but she couldn't stop him. She was very sad, and flew away from her nest, making up her mind that she would never build or sing in Jimmy's garden again.

Jimmy went on collecting eggs. He only told Connie about them, and wanted to show them to her, but she wouldn't look. "I think you are bad and unkind," she said. "You are making a lot of birds unhappy. I don't like you."

One day Jimmy walked by the old ruined castle. He heard the sound of many birds crying "chack-chack-chack" and he looked up.

"What a lot of jackdaws!" he said to himself. "Oh – wouldn't I like some jackdaws' eggs! I know I could find some if I climbed up to see."

It wasn't very difficult for Jimmy to climb up to the castle tower. He found footholds in the crumbling stone, and made his way up little by little. Soon he found himself looking through a hole, inside which a jackdaw had built his enormous untidy nest of twigs.

And there, just within reach of Jimmy's hand, were three big eggs. "What a bit of luck!" said Jimmy, and he put out his hand to take them.

Soon he was climbing down the walls again, the eggs safely in his pocket. He hurried home, and found a box big enough to put the eggs in. He really had quite a

fine collection now! He took all the eggs every time he found a nest – he did not leave the mother bird even one or two. He did not think once of her sadness when she found she had no eggs left to sit on.

The next day Jimmy was sitting in his room by the open window, drawing a map of England for his geography lesson. He was using his lovely bright silver pencil, of course.

He got up to fetch his ruler, and put his pencil down on the window ledge. Just as he did this, a big bird, quite black except for a grey patch at the back of its head and neck, came flying by.

It was a jackdaw. It saw the silver pencil shining in the sun and it flew down to the sill at once. It loved bright, shiny things.

It picked the silver pencil up in its beak. It was heavy, but the jackdaw was a big, strong bird. Jimmy turned when he heard the flutter of wings.

He saw the jackdaw pick up his precious pencil. He saw him fly off with it in his beak! He saw him getting smaller and smaller as he flew right away to the castle tower, where he and the other jackdaws had their nests!

"Oh!" shouted Jimmy. "Oh! You wicked bird! You've stolen my pencil! Come back, come back!"

But the jackdaw didn't come back. He put it into his nest. He already had a piece of silver paper there and somebody's shining thimble. The pencil looked nice laid beside them.

Jimmy was terribly upset. He ran to the window and yelled. He began to cry, and the tears ran down his cheeks like two little streams. He was still crying when Connie came into his room.

"That jackdaw is a thief!" wailed Jimmy. "He has stolen my most precious

thing – the silver pencil I loved."

Connie looked at Jimmy, and didn't say anything.

"Why don't you say something?" cried Jimmy, wiping his tears. "You know how much I loved my pencil. I won it for a prize. Aren't you sorry it's gone? It's most unfair of that jackdaw to come and take it like that."

"Well, I think it was fair, not unfair,"

said Connie, at last. "After all, Jimmy, the jackdaw was doing exactly the same thing you did to him. You took his eggs – and he took your pencil."

"But I loved my pencil!" cried Jimmy.

"Birds love their eggs," said Connie. "They wouldn't sit so long on them as they do, they wouldn't look so happy when they are sitting, if they didn't love their eggs. That little hedge-sparrow loved her eggs, but you took them. The robin loved hers, and you took them. The jackdaw did too, but you took those."

"But my pencil was made of silver and it was very precious," wept Jimmy.

"I expect birds' eggs are even more precious to them than your silver pencil was to you," said Connie. "After all, eggs have something alive in them – baby birds. I expect they are as precious to the bird as you are to your mother."

"Connie, be nice to me, I am so unhappy," said Jimmy.

"I would be nice to you if you could see that what has happened is quite fair and just," said Connie. "You said the jackdaw was wicked because he stole your pencil.

Well, why can't you see that you were bad to steal his eggs? You do horrid things yourself – but you don't like it when the same kind of thing happens to you. And what is more, I don't think the jackdaw is wicked, because he doesn't know that stealing is wrong, and you do!"

"Oh, Connie, I do see that it's fair and just," wept poor Jimmy. "I do, I do. I won't take any more eggs. I was greedy and horrid to take every egg I saw. I won't do it any more. I know what it's like now to be without something I love. Oh, I wish I hadn't been so horrid."

Connie put her arms round him. "Don't cry," she said. "I'll be nice to you now you say that. Perhaps I could buy you a new pencil with the money out of my money-box."

"No, don't do that," said Jimmy at once. "Perhaps the jackdaw will bring my pencil back."

But he didn't. It is still in his nest. Poor Jimmy! It was a hard punishment, but a very fair one, wasn't it?

The
Whistling Pig

Once upon a time there was a very strange pig. His body was made of a balloon, and on to it were stuck four legs, a curly tail and a tiny head. When Jimmy blew him up he looked fine – for he had a great fat body then, and he stood squarely on his four legs like a real little pig.

When Jimmy took out the little cork from the pig's snout, the air came out of him, and his fat balloon body went down to nothing. As he went small, he whistled – such a sad, piercing whistle, like a very high whine. Then he fell over and lay still.

"He's dead!" said Jimmy. "Now I'll make him alive again!" So he blew him up and stood him on his feet once more, a fat and jolly pig.

He took him to the playroom and stood him on the windowsill. Then he went to get ready for bed, for it was seven o'clock.

The pig stood on the windowsill, and, when the toys came out of the cupboard to play, they talked to him. They did like him – he was such a jolly chap, full of jokes and fun.

He told them stories of the toyshop he had come from. He told them about a beautiful fairy doll who had sat next to him on the shelf there, and had been sold to go on the top of the biggest Christmas tree in the town. He was soon their very

best friend, and even the clockwork mouse, who was a very timid creature, would tell the pig his troubles – how his key was always being lost, and how Jimmy had once stepped on his tail and broken a small piece off.

The toys had one serious trouble indeed – and that was a horrid little gnome who lived in the garden below, and often came into the playroom to tease and torment them. How they hated him!

"He tore my new sash," said the big doll.

"He pulled off all my whiskers," said the big rabbit, sorrowfully.

"He pulled off one of my wheels," said the engine. "Now I don't run properly."

"He may come tonight," said the black doll. "He usually does when the moon is full."

And sure enough he came! The pig saw him slip in at the window, a nasty, ugly little creature. When he saw the pig he looked surprised, for he had never seen him before. He gave his tail a sharp pull.

Then down on the floor he jumped and ran to tease the toys. He pulled the

clockwork mouse's tail in half. He tore out some of the black doll's hair – and then he took hold of the poor little baby doll, who was so frightened that she couldn't even cry for help!

The little pig had watched everything. When he saw how scared the baby doll was, he boiled with rage. He leaped down

119

on the floor and jigged about on his four legs, in front of the gnome.

"Leave the doll alone, leave her alone!" he cried.

"Hello, funny face!" said the rude gnome. And then, what do you suppose he did? He took hold of the cork in the pig's snout – the one that kept the air in him – and pulled it out!

"I'm dying again, I'm dying again!" cried the pig sorrowfully. "Now I shan't be able to help the baby doll!"

As the air rushed out of his fat body he began to make his loud, whining, whistling noise. How loud it was in the night! All the toys scampered back to the cupboard in fright, for they felt sure that someone would hear the noise. The gnome stared at the pig in fear. How could he possibly make such a terrible noise? And what was happening to him? He was getting smaller and smaller – and then at last he fell over, *flump*, on the ground, and lay there, quite still.

"I've killed him," said the gnome, frightened.

Just then the door opened – and in came Jimmy! He had been awakened by the pig's whistling noise, and had come to see what all the excitement was.

He didn't see the little pig lying flat on the carpet – but he saw the gnome trying to creep round in shadows to get out of the window. Jimmy thought he was a rat.

The little boy caught up his cricket bat and hit out at what he thought was the rat. He caught the gnome on his legs, *thwack*! And again – *thwack*! Oooh! How that gnome screeched! He leaped out of the window in a flash, and Jimmy stared in surprise as he went – for in the moonlight he certainly didn't look like a rat!

"Well, whoever you are, you won't come back again in a hurry!" said Jimmy, and went back to bed.

When he had gone, the toys ran out of the cupboard again, and stood round the poor little flat pig.

"He was so brave," said the black doll.

"He was so kind," said the baby doll.

"He was the nicest toy of all," said the teddy bear, and began to cry.

"Now he's dead and won't be able to talk to us any more!" said the mouse.

The pig moved himself a little and spoke in a voice like a breath.

"Don't be silly! I'm not really dead! I'm meant to go flat like this and make a noise! Doll, blow me up!"

How joyful the toys were to hear him speak! The doll put his mouth to the pig's snout and blew. The pig swelled a little. The doll blew again. The pig swelled a little more. Then the teddy had a turn. He had a good deal of breath, so he blew the pig up quite fat. But he wasn't yet fat enough to stand on his legs. So the big doll had a turn and she blew him up well. He stood on his legs and grinned at everyone.

"Put my cork in, quick!" he said. "I shall begin to make that awful whistling noise again if you don't."

"Here's the cork," said the mouse, who had seen it on the carpet. The doll fixed it carefully into the pig's snout. There he

was, fat and well and jolly again!

"Did you see Jimmy whack that gnome?" said the pig, pleased. "My, it was a fine sight! He won't come here again!"

"It was clever of you to wake up Jimmy," all the toys said gratefully. "We'll make you king, little pig – and the big doll shall make you a little golden crown to wear! We do love you so much!"

So now the whistling pig wears a small crown. Jimmy can't think where it has come from. Once he took it off the pig and put it on the clockwork mouse – but the next morning it was back on the pig again!

As for that horrid gnome, he hasn't been heard of since!

Funny Little
Mankie

Mankie was a funny little cat without a tail. She was a Manx cat, which was why she was called Mankie. She had just a stump where her tail should be, as all Manx cats have.

At first, when she was only a kitten, she kept to the house and garden. She was afraid to go very far. She was even afraid of the dead leaves that bounded about in the wind!

She didn't know any other animals at all. Sometimes she put her head round the playroom door and looked at the toys there, but when the ball bounced over to her she was frightened and fled away.

Then, when she grew bigger, she got bolder – and one night, when she put her head round the playroom door, the toys called to her. "Come along in. Who are

125

you? What's your name?"

"I'm Mankie," said the little cat, and came right in.

"She's a mankie," said the toys to one another. "What's a mankie?"

Nobody knew. "Well – I'm a monkey, but she's nothing like me," said the toy monkey. "My tail is much, much longer than the mankie's."

"How long is your tail?" the clown asked Mankie. "Turn round with your back to us and let us see. If you've got a long tail you can swing by, you may be a kind of monkey, not a mankie."

Mankie turned and the toys all

exclaimed loudly, "Why, you haven't got a tail!"

"Where's your tail?"

"Have you lost it?"

Mankie was astonished. She had never even thought about tails before. She looked at Monkey's beautiful long one. She looked at the toy dog's short one, and the toy horse's long hairy one. Then she looked at herself.

"My tail certainly isn't there," she said sadly. "I must have dropped it somewhere."

The toys thought that was quite likely.

"The horse lost his tail once," said the clown. "It came unstuck and dropped out. He didn't notice it for a long time, and he spent all night long looking for it."

"Hrrrumph," said the big rocking-horse, suddenly, making everyone jump. "My tail went too, once. A naughty boy pulled it right out. My word, I did feel cold without it!"

"Do you feel cold behind, little mankie?" said the clown.

"Perhaps I do, a bit," said Mankie. "Oh, dear – goodness knows where I've dropped my tail. It might be anywhere in the house!"

"If this mankie had a tail, she would be rather like a cat," said the toy horse. "Let's all go and look for her tail."

So they all slipped out of the playroom and went down the stairs to hunt for Mankie's tail. Mankie went too.

"What's your tail like?" asked the clown. "Is it black or white, or what?"

Mankie thought hard. "I don't know," she said at last. "I've never noticed."

"Did you ever swing yourself upside down by it, like this?" said the toy monkey, and suddenly leaped up to the banister and hung himself upside down by his tail. Mankie stared in surprise.

"Oh no. I'm sure I never hung myself up by my tail," she said. "I would have noticed that, I'm sure." They met a little mouse down in the hall. He ran into his hole, and then peeped out, only his little black nose showing.

"Mouse! Have you found a tail lying about anywhere?" asked the toy monkey.

"No. Indeed I haven't," said the mouse. "Why, who has lost one?"

"This animal here – a mankie," said the monkey. The mouse stared at Mankie and got further down his hole. "Looks like a cat to me, not a mankie," he said in fright. "Anyway, it's not having my tail!" And away down his hole he went, his long thin tail behind him.

"Silly mouse," said the clown. "As if anyone wants his skinny tail! Come on – we'll go to the kitchen and see if the window's open. If it is we'll go and ask the dog if he's seen your tail anywhere."

The dog was next door's dog. Mankie had heard him bark but she hadn't seen him. She was afraid of this big creature in his kennel. The toys pushed her forward.

"Rover! Have you seen a mankie tail about anywhere?" asked the toy dog. "This creature here, a mankie, has lost one!"

Rover stared at Mankie, who began to shiver in fright. "Dear me, do you feel cold because you've lost your tail?" asked Rover. "Was it a big one that you could wrap yourself up in, like a squirrel's?"

"No, I don't think so," said Mankie. "I don't remember wrapping myself up in it. It couldn't have been a very big tail."

"Let's make sure it's gone," said Rover, and he laughed when Mankie turned her back on him. "Good gracious! You've just a stump, that's all. Are you sure nobody's bitten it off?"

"I'm quite sure of that!" said Mankie. "I'd have felt somebody biting it off."

"Was it a tail anything like mine?" asked Rover, and he suddenly came right out of his kennel and stood with his back to Mankie. He wagged his big tail so fast

that he knocked both the monkey and the
clown right over!

"Good gracious!" said Mankie, in
astonishment. "What a wonderful tail!
I'd like one like that!"

"Yes. It's got a very, very good wag in it,
hasn't it?" said Rover, pleased. "You can't
get tails like that in a hurry!"

131

"Well, I wouldn't mind a smaller one if it had a good wag," said Mankie. "Where can I get one? I know I shall never, never find mine."

Rover lay down in his kennel and thought. "You might go to the little imp who lives in the cucumber frame," he said. "There aren't any cucumbers there now, because it's wintertime, so you'll easily find him. His name's Snorty. He knows a wonderful lot of magic."

"Yes. His mother was the servant of a wizard," said the clown. "He told me. Snorty might be able to grow a new tail for the mankie."

So they all went off to find Snorty. He was certainly in the cucumber frame because they could hear him snoring!

"His name should be Snorey, not Snorty," said the clown, with a giggle, and he rapped on the glass of the frame.

Snorty woke up and squeezed out of a broken pane of glass. He looked in surprise at the toys. "Hello," he said. "What's all this, in the middle of the night?"

"We've come to ask you if you can grow a new tail on this mankie," replied

the clown. "She's lost hers, and we can't find it anywhere."

Snorty looked at Mankie and gave a little snort. "What a peculiar creature – a bit like a cat. What sort of a tail did she have?"

"She doesn't know," said the monkey.

"Then I can't grow her a new tail," said Snorty.

"Well, I'll have a tail like Rover's, with a wag in it," said Mankie.

133

"Oh, no you won't," said Snorty, with a bigger snort. "That would take up almost all the magic I've got. Anyway, what's the use of a big wag to you? You'd fall over every time you wagged your tail!"

"I wouldn't," said Mankie, crossly.

"Now, don't squabble," said the toy horse. "What about a smaller tail, Snorty?"

"I tell you, I can't grow the mankie a tail unless I know exactly what a mankie tail is like," said Snorty. "That's my last word." He began to climb back into the cucumber frame, but the clown caught hold of his collar.

"No. Wait a minute," he said. "If you can't grow a new tail, you can surely get back her old one for her! You know enough magic for that."

"All right, all right," said Snorty. "I've a come-back spell somewhere. I'll give it to the mankie. If she swallows it, her tail will come slithering up to her out of the darkness, and she'll have it again!"

He felt in his pockets and brought out a little yellow pill that shone strangely in the moonlight. "Here you are," he said to Mankie. "It's got a come-back spell in it. Swallow it, think hard of tails, and your own will come back to you, no matter where you left it."

Mankie swallowed the strange yellow pill. Everyone waited for the tail to come back, but it didn't. Once the clown gave a shout because he thought it was coming, but it was only a worm in the grass.

After they had waited for five minutes they called out to Snorty, who had gone back to his home in the cucumber frame. "Hey, Snorty! The tail hasn't come back. Your spell's no good."

Snorty was very angry. He threw

showers of earth out of the hole in the glass over everyone. "How dare you say my spell is no good! It's a very powerful one. Go away, you ungrateful creatures!"

Very sadly they all went back home. On the way they met the big black cat from next door. He stared in surprise.

"It's all right. It's only us," said the monkey. "We got a come-back spell from Snorty to get back this mankie's tail – but the spell was a failure. The tail didn't come back."

"Snorty's spells are never failures," said the black cat. "The mankie couldn't have had a tail. Whoever heard of a mankie or its tail? Where's this strange creature?"

The moon sailed out from behind a cloud. The toys pushed Mankie forward.

"Look – this is the mankie, who lost her tail." The big black cat looked and looked. Then he laughed with a loud yowl that frightened all the toys.

"He-hee-hee-ow-hee-ow! That's not a mankie – it's a cat. A Manx cat without a tail! Manx cats never do have tails, didn't you know that? No wonder the come-back spell was no good. A mankie

indeed – she's just a cat like me! I knew her mother and she didn't have a tail either! He-hee-hee-ow!"

Well, well, well! Mankie and the toys were most astonished. The clown was cross with Mankie. "You told us you were a mankie and had lost your tail," he said. "And you're not. You're just an ordinary cat that hasn't got one."

"I said my name was Mankie!" wept poor Mankie. "I didn't say I *was* a mankie – and it was you who told me I'd lost my tail! Oh, dear, oh, dear – now I'll never, never have one!"

And poor Mankie rushed indoors and curled up in her basket, very miserable indeed. But when she heard next day that Rover had chased the big black cat and nipped the top off his tail, she couldn't help feeling that after all it was a very, very good thing that she hadn't got one!

She went to tell the toys this and they agreed, too. The monkey asked the clown to tie his tail safely round his middle, just in case he met Rover that day.

"I'm glad that I haven't got a tail," said Mankie. "It might be such a nuisance. I'd have to be sure I didn't lose the wag out of it. I'd have to see that Rover didn't bite it. And if I swung upside down on it like Monkey does, I might fall and bump my head. I'm very, very glad I haven't got a tail."

Have you ever seen a Manx cat? They're just like Mankie, without a tail at all!

The Little
Prickly Family

Once upon a time all the animals in Fir Tree Wood lived together in peace and happiness. There were the rabbits and the toads, the hedgehogs and the mice, the squirrels and the moles, and many others.

Then one day King Loppy, the sandy rabbit, sat down on what he thought was a brown heap of leaves – but it was Mr Prickles the hedgehog. He didn't like being sat on, and he stuck all his sharp spines upright, so that King Loppy jumped up with a shout of pain.

"How dare you prick the King of the Wood?" cried Loppy, standing his ears up straight in his anger. "You did it on purpose!"

"No, I didn't, really," said Mr Prickles. "But it's not nice to be sat on quite so hard."

"Well, I banish you from the wood!" said King Loppy, and he pointed with his paw towards the east, where the wood grew thinner. "Go away at once, and take your horrid prickly family with you."

Mr Prickles could do nothing else but obey. So sadly he went to fetch his wife and his six prickly children. They packed up all they owned, and walked out of Fir Tree Wood.

Now they hadn't been gone long when

a family of red goblins came to the wood. They went to the Bluebell Dell, which was a pretty little hollow, and made their home there, right in the very middle of the wood.

At first the creatures of the wood took no notice, but soon the goblins made their lives so miserable that even King Loppy vowed he would turn the goblins out.

But he couldn't! The goblins knew too much magic, and the animals were always afraid to say what they really thought for fear of being turned into mushrooms or earwigs. So they had to put up with their larders being raided each night, their firewood stolen, and their young ones frightened by the dreadful noises and ugly faces that the goblins made.

Once every month, when the moon was full, the goblins did a strange, barefoot dance in the dell. They danced round and round in the moonlight, holding hands and singing loud songs. All the animals were kept awake, and didn't they grumble – but not very loud, in case the red goblins heard and punished them.

"If anyone can get rid of these ugly red

creatures for me, he shall be king instead of me!" declared Loppy one night. "Our lives are a misery now, and these goblins must go!"

Well, a good many of the animals thought they would like to be king and wear the woodland crown, but try as they would, they couldn't think of a plan to make the goblins go.

Frisky the red squirrel wrote them a polite letter, and begged them to leave, but the only reply he had was to see all his nuts stolen one bright moonlight night.

Then Mowdie the mole wrote a very

stern letter, and said that she would get a policeman from the world of humans, and have them all locked up, if they didn't go away, but they came and laughed so loudly at her that she shivered with fright and didn't go out shopping for three days.

Then bold Mr Hare marched right up to the goblins one day and ordered them out of the wood. He took a whip with him, and threatened to beat each goblin if they didn't obey him.

The goblins sat round and smiled. When Mr Hare tried to use his whip he found that he couldn't move! The goblins had used magic, and he was stuck fast to the ground! Then they tied him up to a birch-tree all night long. Loppy found him the next morning, and Mr Hare vowed that he would never go near those horrid red goblins again!

After that no one did anything, till one day a letter came to Loppy from Mr Prickles the hedgehog. He opened it; and this is what it said:

Dear Your Majesty,
    I think I can get rid of the goblins
for you, but I do not want to be king.
I only want to be allowed to come and
live in Fir Tree Wood with all
my friends once more. Please let me.
                    Your loving servant,
                    Prickles

When Loppy had read the letter he sat down and wrote an answer. This is what he said:

Dear Mr Prickles,
    You may come back here to live if you can get rid of the goblins. But I don't believe you can.
                        Your loving king,
                            Loppy

When Mr Prickles got the letter he was overjoyed, for he felt certain he could get rid of the goblins. He looked up his calendar, and found that the next full-moon night was three nights ahead. On that night the red goblins would have their barefoot dance.

That day Mr Prickles went to see Tibbles the pixie, who was a great friend of his.

"I want you to do something for me," he said. "Will you go to the red goblins in Fir Tree Wood and tell them that someone has sent you to warn them against the magic pins and needles?"

"Goodness!" said Tibbles, with a laugh.

146

"What a funny message – and whatever are the pins and needles?"

"Never mind about that," said Mr Prickles. "You just go and give that message, there's a good pixie, and you can come back and have tea with us."

So Tibbles set off to Bluebell Dell, and when he saw the red goblins he gave them the message.

"Someone has sent me to give you a warning," he said, in a very solemn voice. "You are to beware of the magic pins and needles."

"Ooh!" said the goblins, looking scared. "What are they? And what will they do? And who told you to warn us?"

"I can answer no questions," said

147

Tibbles, and he walked off, leaving the goblins wondering whatever the message meant.

Now, when the night of the full moon came, Mr Prickles and his wife and family made their way to Bluebell Dell. The red goblins were already beginning their barefoot dance. Their shoes and stockings were laid in a neat pile under a tree.

Without being seen, Mrs Prickles went to the pile, picked them up, and took them to the lily-pond not far off. She dropped all the shoes and stockings into the water, and then went back to her family.

"Are you all ready?" whispered Mr Prickles. "Then – *roll*!"

With one accord all the hedgehogs curled themselves up tightly into balls, and rolled down the dell to the bottom where the goblins were busy dancing. They rolled all among their feet, and soon there was a terrible shouting and crying.

"Ooh! Ooh! I've trodden on a thorn! I've trodden on a prickle! Ooh! What's this!"

The hedgehogs rolled themselves in and out, and the goblins couldn't help treading on them. The prickles ran into their bare feet, and they hopped about in pain.

"What is it? What is it?" they cried; but at that moment the moon went in, and the goblins couldn't see anything. They just went on treading on the prickly

hedgehogs, and cried out in pain and fright.

Then the head goblin suddenly gave a cry of dismay, "It must be the magic pins and needles! It must be! We were warned against them, we were told to beware! Quick, put on your shoes and stockings before we get into their power!"

But the goblins couldn't find their pile of shoes and stockings – and no wonder, for they were all down at the bottom of the pond. They ran here and there looking for them, and Mr Hedgehog and his family rolled here and there after them. How those hedgehogs enjoyed themselves!

"The pins and needles have taken our shoes!" cried the goblins. "Oh, oh, what shall we do? The pins and needles have found us!"

"Quick!" cried the head goblin. "We must go back to Goblin Town and buy some more shoes for our feet. We must never come back here again!"

Off the goblins ran, as fast as they could, and the hedgehogs rolled after them. If any goblin stopped to take breath he at once felt a prickly something on his foot,

and he gave a cry of fright and ran on.

They made such a noise that all the wood animals came out to see what was the matter; and just then the moon shone out. The surprised animals saw the red goblins running for their lives, with the whole of the little prickly family of hedgehogs after them!

When the goblins were really gone,

everyone crowded round the hedgehogs.

"You brave things to chase away those goblins!" cried Loppy the king. "How could you dare to do such a thing! You are very plucky, Mr Prickles."

"He shall be king!" shouted the animals.

"No," said Mr Prickles, modestly. "I am not great enough to be king. Loppy is far better than I am; but, please, Your Majesty, may I come back to live here, with all my prickly family?"

"Of course!" Loppy said gladly. "But do tell me – how did you manage to chase the goblins away, Mr Prickles?"

"That is a secret," said the hedgehog, and he wouldn't say another word.

Then he and all his prickly family came back to their home in the wood again and were very happy. Everyone praised them, and King Loppy had them to tea once a week, so you see he had quite forgiven Mr Prickles for having pricked him when he sat down upon him.

As for the red goblins, they were never heard of again, but folk do say that whenever they think of that last moonlight night in Fir Tree Wood they get a funny feeling in their feet, and then they say:

"Ooh, I've got pins and needles!"

Have you ever felt that way too?

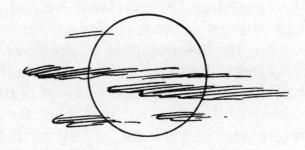

Well Done,
Bob-Along!

Whenever anyone in Brownie Town had a party they always went shopping at Mr Knobbly's shop. He was a brownie with bright green eyes and such bony arms and legs that really Knobbly was a very good name for him.

"Everything for parties!" Knobbly would call out whenever any of the little folk went by. "Balloons of all colours, big and bouncy, blown up as large as you like. Funny hats for everyone – buy a bonnet for Mr Grumble, buy a dunce's hat for the schoolmaster! Crackers to pull with the biggest bang you ever heard!"

It was a lovely shop to wander round. Balloons bumped against your head, pretty lanterns swung to and fro, funny hats could be tried on, and shining ornaments glittered everywhere.

All the same, nobody liked Knobbly very much. He was a cheat, and when anybody ordered two dozen balloons, he would send only twenty-two or twenty-three, and hope that nobody would bother to count them. And often some of his crackers had nothing in them, and that was very disappointing indeed.

One day Knobbly was very, very pleased. Mr Popple, the richest brownie in the town, was giving a big party for his little girl, Peronel, and, of course, he had been to order a great many things from Knobbly's shop.

"I want one hundred balloons," he

said. "And twelve boxes of coloured crackers, each with a nice little present inside. And one hundred funny hats, with strong elastic for each one, so that the children can keep them on easily. I'll pay you well, so be sure and see that everything is first class."

"Certainly, Mr Popple, sir, certainly," said Knobbly, too delighted for words. "When is this party, sir?"

"In one week's time," said Popple. "All the balloons must be blown up very big, and have nice long strings, and be delivered on the morning of the party, so that they can be hung up all round the room."

Knobbly was soon very, very busy. He made a great many funny hats, and indeed he was very clever at that. But he wasn't going to put good strong elastic on them – oh no – strong elastic was expensive – he would get very cheap stuff. Nobody would notice!

"And I'm not going to put presents into each cracker, either," said Knobbly to himself. "Often when a cracker is pulled, the present is shot out and goes under the table or somewhere! If a cracker has no present in it, the child will think it's flown right out and go and look for it. He won't know that he'll never find it because it wasn't there! Ha, ha – I'm a wily brownie, I am!" It was when he came to blow up the balloons that he found himself in difficulties.

He didn't mind blowing up a dozen, he had often done that – but a hundred! He looked at the piles of flat rubber, all balloons waiting to be blown up, and he shook his head.

"No – I can't do it. I'll have to get

157

someone in to help." So he put a notice in his window:

WANTED
SOMEONE TO BLOW UP
BALLOONS

That day a small, rather raggedy brownie came by. He went about doing odd jobs, and he was a merry, honest little fellow that everybody liked. He saw the notice and popped his head round the door. "I can blow up balloons," he said. "I've plenty of good breath, available at any moment of the day. I can also put a whistle into any balloon when I blow it up."

"What do you mean?" said Knobbly, surprised.

"Well, I whistle as I blow," said the brownie, "and naturally, when I fill a balloon with my breath and whistle at the same time, the whistle goes into the balloon too – and when it's going down, as balloons do sooner or later, it whistles to warn the owner to blow it up again!"

"How extraordinary!" said Knobbly, thinking that he could certainly charge extra for whistling balloons. "All right, you can have the job. What's your name?"

"Bob-Along," said the brownie. "And I'm honest as the day, as anyone will tell you. What will you pay me?"

"Depends on your work," said Knobbly. "Now look – fasten elastic on these hats for me, before you begin on the balloons."

Bob-Along fixed elastic on a clown's hat and then popped it on. But the elastic broke at once.

"Hey," said Bob-Along, "this elastic's no good. Give me stronger pieces."

159

"You just do as you're told," said Knobbly, who was busy making crackers. Bob-Along picked one up. It was very pretty indeed. He shook it.

"Nothing inside!" he said, and took a toy and pushed it into the cracker.

"You stop that," said Knobbly crossly. "I'm doing the crackers!"

Bob-Along watched him. "Well, you're not doing them very well," he said, after a minute or two. "You've missed putting toys into two more crackers. Better let me put the toys in for you, while you make them."

"You blow up the balloons," said Knobbly, getting tired of being watched by this bright-eyed brownie. "Another word from you and I'll kick you out of my shop!"

"You won't," said Bob-Along. "You haven't any breath to blow up your balloons! I've plenty! I'll start on them now, whistle and all!"

Well, Bob-Along certainly did know how to blow up balloons steadily and well. He whistled as he blew, and showed Knobbly how his whistle came out of the balloon

160

again when he let the air out of it. It was really very peculiar. Knobbly was pleased, and decided to charge even more for them than he had planned at first.

More and more balloons were blown up by Bob-Along, and he tied each one's neck with a piece of string, and hung it to a pole, so that it did not get entangled with the others. Soon there were thirty hanging up, bobbing about gaily.

"Shall I shake each cracker for you, and see if you've left out any toys?" asked Bob-Along. "I want a rest from blowing now. I

never blow up more than thirty balloons at a time, in case I use up all my breath."

"Don't be silly," said Knobbly. "If you feel like that you can come back tomorrow – but they'll have to be finished then, because that's the day of the party."

Bob-Along finished all the balloons the next day, and then, as Knobbly bade him, took them to Popple's big house. Mr Popple was very, very pleased with such big ones, especially when he knew that a whistle had been blown into each one. Then Bob-Along went back to Knobbly's.

"I want my money, please," he said.

"Here you are – fifty pence," said Knobbly, and threw the money on the table.

"What – fifty pence for my excellent work?" cried Bob-Along. "I want three pounds – and that's cheap for what I did."

"You'll take fifty pence or nothing," said Knobbly, making the last cracker.

"Then I'll take nothing – except what I've put into your balloons!" said Bob-Along, and marched out.

"Hey – what do you mean?" cried Knobbly, but Bob-Along didn't answer. He went straight to Mr Popple's and slipped into the party room, where the hundred balloons swung and swayed.

He untied the neck of the first one and then another. The air came out with a loud whistle and the balloons went flat. Then Bob-Along undid three more, and again the air came whistling out. Mr Popple heard the noise and came running in. "Look here – what are you doing?" he cried. "You've blown all those up – why

are you making them flat again? You've been paid for that work!"

"No, I haven't," said Bob-Along. "Knobbly offered me fifty pence, and I wouldn't take such a poor sum. So I've come to take away my breath – the breath I put into each balloon, and the whistle too. They're mine – my breath and my whistle – and if I'm not going to be paid for them, I'll have them back!"

"You dishonest fellow!" cried Mr Popple.

"Oh no, I'm not!" said Bob-Along. "It's Knobbly that's dishonest! You ask him how many crackers he's not put toys into! You try on one of his funny hats and see how the elastic snaps at once. Well, he may trick you – but he's not going to trick me!"

"Wait!" said Popple. "Come down to Knobbly's with me. I'll soon get your money for you!" And away he went with Bob-Along grinning beside him. What a shock Knobbly had when they walked into his shop. Popple shook all the crackers and found that nineteen of them were empty! He tried on three funny hats and each time the elastic snapped almost at once.

"Ha! And you wouldn't pay a fair wage to this good worker here!" shouted Popple. "Wait till I get my wand! I'll

wish you away to the darkest cave in the mountains, you dishonest brownie!"

But Knobbly didn't wait. He took to his heels and fled, and never came back again. And Bob-Along quickly put strong elastic on to the hats and filled the empty crackers, and blew up the flat balloons – and went to the party too!

And who do you suppose has Knobbly's shop now? Yes, little Bob-Along, with his merry face and honest ways. Well, he deserves to have it, doesn't he?

Winkle-Pip
Walks Out

Once upon a time Winkle-Pip the gnome
did a good turn to the Tappetty Witch,
and she was very grateful. "I will give you
something," she said. "Would you like a
wishing-suit?"

"Oooh, yes please!" cried Winkle-Pip,
delighted. "That would be lovely."

So the Tappetty Witch gave Winkle-Pip
a wishing-suit. It was made of yellow silk,
spotted with red, and had big pockets in it.

"Now," said the witch to Winkle-Pip,
"whenever you wear this suit, your wishes
will come true – but there is one thing you
must do, Winkle."

"What's that?" asked Winkle-Pip.

"Once a year you must go out into the
world of boys and girls and grant wishes
to six of them," said the witch. "Now
don't forget that, Winkle, or the magic

will go out of your wishing-suit."

Winkle-Pip promised not to forget, and off he went home, with the wishing-suit wrapped up in brown paper, tucked safely under his arm.

Now the next day Winkle-Pip's old Aunt Maria was coming to see him. She always liked a very good tea, and often grumbled because Winkle-Pip, who was not a very good cook, sometimes gave her burnt cakes, or a sponge cake which hadn't risen well, and was all wet and heavy.

So the gnome decided to use his wishing-suit the next day, and give his aunt a wonderful surprise. He put it on in the morning and looked at himself in the glass – and he looked very nice indeed. He thought he would try the wish-magic, so he put his hands in his pockets and spoke aloud.

"I wish for a fine feathered cap to go with my suit!" he said.

Hey presto! A yellow hat with a red feather came from nowhere and landed with a thud on his big head.

"Ho!" said Winkle-Pip, pleased. "That's a real beauty."

He looked round his kitchen. It was not very clean, and none of the breakfast dishes had been washed up. The curtains looked dirty too, and Winkle-Pip remembered that his Aunt Maria had said he really should wash them.

"Now for a bit of fun!" said Winkle, and he put his hands in his pockets again.

"Kitchen, tidy yourself, for that is my wish!" he said loudly.

At once things began to stir and

hum. The tap ran water and the dishes jumped about in the bowl and washed themselves. The cloth jumped out of the pail under the sink, and rubbed itself hard on the soap. Then it began to wash the kitchen floor far more quickly than Winkle-Pip had ever been able to do.

The brush leaped out of its corner and

swept the rugs, which were really very dirty indeed. The pan held itself ready for the sweepings, and when it was full it ran outside to the dustbin, and emptied itself there.

You should have seen the kitchen when everything had quietened down again! How it shone and glittered! Even the saucepans had joined in and had let themselves be scrubbed well in the sink. It was marvellous.

"Now for the curtains!" said Winkle-Pip, and he put his hands in his pockets again. "I wish you to make yourselves clean!" he called.

The curtains didn't need to be told twice. They sprang off their hooks and rushed to the sink. The tap ran and filled the basin with hot water. The soap made a lather, and then those curtains jumped themselves up and down in the water until every speck of dirt had run from them and they were as white as snow! Then they flew to the mangle, which squeezed the water from them. Then out to the line in the yard they went, and the pegs pegged them there in the wind. The wind blew its hardest, and in a few minutes they flew back into the kitchen once more. The iron had already put itself on the stove to heat, and as soon as the curtains appeared and laid themselves flat on the table, the iron jumped over to them and ironed them beautifully.

Then back to their hooks they flew, and hung themselves at the windows. How lovely they looked!

"Wonderful!" cried Winkle-Pip in delight. "My, I wonder what my old Aunt Maria will say!"

Then he began to think about food.

"I think I'll have a big chocolate cake, a jelly with sliced pears in it, little ginger cakes, some ham sandwiches, some fresh lettuce and radishes, and some raspberries and cream," decided Winkle. "That would make a simply glorious tea!"

So he wished for all of those – and you should just have seen his kitchen coming to life again. It didn't take the magic very long to make all the cakes and sandwiches he wanted, and to wash the lettuce and radishes that suddenly flew in from the garden.

"Splendid!" cried the gnome, clapping his hands with joy. "Won't my Aunt Maria stare to see all this?"

In the afternoon his old aunt came – and as soon as she opened the kitchen door, how she stared! She looked at the snowy sink, she looked at the spotless floor. She stared at the clean curtains, and she stared at the shining saucepans. Then she gazed at the lovely tea spread out on the table.

"Well!" she cried in astonishment. "What a marvellous change, Winkle-Pip. How hard you must have worked! I really am very, very pleased with you."

She gave the gnome a loud kiss, and he blushed very red.

"It's my wishing-suit, Aunt," he said, for he was a truthful little gnome. He told her all about it and she was full of surprise.

"Well, you be sure to take great care of it," she said, eating a big piece of chocolate cake. "And whatever you do, Winkle-Pip, don't forget to go out into the world of boys and girls and find six of them to grant wishes to – or you'll lose the wishing-magic as sure as eggs are eggs."

Winkle-Pip did enjoy his wishing-suit! He granted wishes to all his friends – and you may be sure that everyone wanted to be his friend when they knew about his new magic suit! Then a time came when he knew that he must go out into our world, for the magic in his suit began to weaken.

So one day Winkle-Pip put on his suit of yellow silk and his fine feathered cap, and

174

walked to the end of Fairyland.

"How pleased all the boys and girls will be to see me!" he said. "And how glad they will be to have their wishes granted. I am sure they don't see fairy folk very often, and they will go mad with joy to find me walking up to them."

"Don't be too sure," said his friend the green pixie, who had walked to the gates of Fairyland with him. "I have heard that the boys and girls nowadays don't believe in fairies, and are much too busy to want to listen to tales about us. They might not believe in you!"

"Rubbish!" said Winkle. He shook hands with the green pixie and walked out into our world. He looked all around him and wondered which way to go.

"I'll go eastwards," he thought. "It looks as if there might be a town over there."

So off he went and after a few miles he came to a little market town. He went along, peeping into the windows of the houses as he passed by, and at last he saw two little girls playing with a beautiful doll's-house, and they were talking about it.

"You know, this doll's-house is very old-fashioned," said one little girl. "It's got oil-lamps, instead of electric light. It's a silly doll's-house, I think."

"Well, I'm sure Grandpa won't have electric light put into it for us," said the other little girl. "I do so wish he would. That would be great."

"Ha!" thought Winkle-Pip. "Here's a chance for me to give them a wish."

So he jumped into the window, and walked quietly up behind the children. "Would you like electric light in that doll's-house?" he asked. "You only have to wish for it, while I am here, and you shall have it."

The children looked round in surprise.

"Of course I'd like it," said the first little girl. "I wish I could have electric light all over the house!"

In a second the magic had worked, and the doll's-house was lit up with tiny electric lights from top to bottom! How the children gasped to see such a wonderful sight. They found that there were tiny switches beside each door, and when they snapped these on and off the lights went on or out. They began to play with them in great excitement.

Meanwhile the gnome stood behind them, waiting for a word of thanks. The

children seemed quite to have forgotten him. He was terribly hurt, and at last he crept out of the window, without even saying goodbye.

"Fancy not thanking me for granting their wish!" he thought, mournfully. "Well, that was a nasty surprise for me! I thought the children would be delighted to talk to me, too."

Winkle-Pip went on again, and after a while he came across two boys hunting in the grass for something they had lost.

"Where can that money have gone?" he heard one of them say. "Oh, I do wish we could find it, for we shall get into such trouble for losing it when we get home."

Up went Winkle-Pip to them. "I can grant you your wish," he said. "I am a gnome, and have my wishing-suit on."

The two boys looked at him.

"Don't be silly," said one. "You know quite well that there are no such things as gnomes – and as for wishing-suits, well, you must think us stupid to believe in things like that! You couldn't possibly grant us a wish!"

Winkle-Pip went very red. He stuck his hands in his pockets and looked at the two boys.

"Do you really want to find that money?" he asked.

"Yes, rather!" said the boys. "We wish we could, for we shall get into trouble for coming home without it."

No sooner had they wished than the money rose up from where it had been hidden in the grass, and flew into Winkle-Pip's hand.

"Here it is," he said to the boys, and gave it to them. But were they pleased? No, not a bit of it!

"You had it all the time!" they cried, for they had not seen it fly into the gnome's hand. "You have played a trick on us! We will chase you."

They set upon the poor gnome and he had to run for his life. He sat down on the first gate he came to to get his breath back.

"Well!" he thought miserably. "That's two wishes granted and not a word of thanks for either of them. What is the world coming to, I wonder? Is there any politeness or gratitude left?"

After a while he went on again, and

soon he heard the sound of sobbing. He peeped round the corner and saw a little girl sitting on the steps of a small house, crying bitterly.

"What's the matter?" asked Winkle-Pip, his kind heart touched by her loud sobs. At first the little girl didn't answer, but just frowned at him. Then suddenly from the house there came a voice.

"Now stop that silly crying, Mary! You deserved to be smacked. It was very naughty of you to break your poor dolly like that, just out of temper."

"I shall break her again if I like!" shouted the naughty little girl, jumping to her feet and stamping hard. The gnome was terribly shocked.

"You shouldn't talk like that," he said. "Why, do you know, I came to give you a wish, and—"

"Silly creature, silly creature!" screamed the bad-tempered child, making an ugly face at him. "I wish you'd go away, that's what I wish! I wish you'd run to the other end of the town; then I wouldn't see you any more!"

Well, of course her wish had to come

true and poor Winkle-Pip found himself scurrying off to the other end of the town in a mighty hurry. He was soon very much out of breath again, but not until he was right at the other end of the little town did his feet stop running.

"My goodness!" said Winkle-Pip, sinking down on the grass by the road-side. "What a horrid day I'm having! What nasty children there are nowadays! Three more wishes to give away – and, dear me, I do wish I'd finished, for I'm not enjoying it at all."

As Winkle-Pip sat there, two children came by, a boy and girl.

"Hello, funny-face," said the boy, rudely. "Wherever do you come from?"

"I come from Fairyland," said the gnome. "I am a gnome, as I should think you could guess."

"Pooh!" said the boy. "What rubbish to talk like that! There are no gnomes or fairies."

"Of course not," said the little girl.

"Well, there are," said Winkle-Pip, "and what's more, I'm a rather special gnome. I've come into your world today to give wishes to six children. I've wasted three wishes, and I'm beginning to think there are no children worth bothering about nowadays."

"What, do you mean you can grant wishes to us?" asked the boy. "I don't believe it! Well, I'll try anyway, and we'll see if what you say is true! I wish for a banana, a pear and a pineapple to come and sit on your head!"

Whee-ee-ee-ee-eesh! Through the air came flying a large banana, very ripe, a big pear, and a spiky pineapple. *Plonk!* They all fell on poor Winkle-Pip's head and he groaned in dismay. The children stared in amazement and began to laugh. Then they looked rather scared.

"Oooh!" said the boy. "He must be a gnome, after all, because our wish came true!"

Winkle-Pip was so angry that he couldn't think what to say. The children gave him one more look and then took to their heels and fled, afraid of what the gnome might do to them in revenge.

Poor Winkle-Pip! He was so distressed and so hurt to think that children could play him such a mean trick when he had offered them a wish, that he hardly knew what to do. He tried his best to get the fruit off his head, but it was so firmly stuck there that it would not move.

"Oh dear! oh dear!" wept the gnome. "I shall have to let it all stay there, because I can't have any wishes for myself till I have given away the six wishes to boys and girls."

Presently there came by a little girl carrying a heavy load of wood. She stopped when she saw the gnome, and looked at him in surprise.

"Why are you carrying all those things

on your head?" she asked. "Aren't they dreadfully heavy?"

"Yes," said the gnome with a sigh. "But I can't very well help it." Then he told the little girl all his story, and she was very sorry for him.

"I do wish I could get it off for you," she said. "If I had a wish, I would wish that, and the fruit would fly away."

No sooner had she spoken those words than her wish came true! Off flew the banana, off went the pear, and off jumped the pineapple. They all disappeared with a click, and the gnome shook his head about in joy.

"Hurrah!" he said. "They've gone. Oh, you nice little girl, I'm so glad you wished

that wish. You're the only unselfish child I have met in my journeys today."

"And you're the first person who has ever called me unselfish," said the little girl, with a sigh. "I live with my stepmother, and she is always telling me I am lazy and selfish. I do try so hard not to be."

"Poor child," said Winkle-Pip, thinking it was a dreadful shame to make a little girl carry such a heavy load of wood. "Have you no kind father?"

"No," said the little girl. "I have an aunt though, but since we moved she doesn't know where my stepmother and I live. My stepmother didn't like her because she was kind to me, and wanted me to live with her. She said I was nothing but a little servant to my stepmother, and so I am. I wouldn't mind that a bit, if only she would love me and be kind to me."

Winkle-Pip was nearly in tears when he heard this sad story. "I do wish I could help you," he said. "What a pity your kind aunt isn't here to take you to her home and love you."

"I do wish she was," said the little

girl, lifting the bundle of wood on to her shoulder again – and then she gave a loud cry of delight and dropped it. Winkle-Pip cried out too, for, what do you think – hurrying towards them was the kindest, plumpest woman you could possibly imagine!

"Auntie! Auntie!" cried the little girl. "I was just wishing you were here!"

"Of course," said Winkle-Pip to himself with a smile, "that's the sixth wish! I'd quite forgotten there was still another one to give. Well, I'm very, very glad that this little girl has got the last wish. She used up one wish to set me free from that banana, pear, and pineapple, and she deserves to have one for herself, bless her kind heart!"

"Where have you come from, Auntie?" asked the little girl, hugging the smiling woman round the neck. "Oh, I have missed you so!"

"I've come to fetch you home with me," said her aunt, kissing her. "I've had such a time trying to find out where your stepmother took you. I don't quite know how I got here, but still, here I am, and

you're coming straight home with me, and I'm going to look after you and love you."

"But what about my stepmother?" asked the child.

"Oh, I'll go and see her for you," said the gnome, with a grin. "I'll tell her what I think of her. You go home with your aunt and have a lovely time. I'll take your wood back for you."

So the little girl went off happily, with her aunt holding her tightly by the hand. Winkle-Pip shouldered the bundle of wood and ran off to the little cottage that the child had pointed out to him.

An ugly, bad-tempered-looking woman opened the door, and frowned when she saw Winkle-Pip.

"I've brought you the wood that your little stepdaughter was bringing," said the gnome. "She has gone to live with her aunt."

"Oh, she has, has she?" said the woman, picking up a broom. "Well, I'm sure you've had something to do with that, you interfering little creature! I'll give you such a drubbing!"

She ran at the little gnome, but he stuck

his hands into his pockets, and wished quickly.

"I've given away six wishes!" he said. "Now my wishing-suit is full of magic for me again – so I wish myself back in Fairyland once more!"

Whee-ee-ee-eesh! He was swept up into the air and vanished before the angry woman's eyes. She turned pale with fright and ran inside her cottage and banged the door. She was so terrified that she

never once tried to find out where her stepdaughter had gone.

As for Winkle-Pip, he was delighted to get home again.

Over a cup of cocoa he told the green pixie all his adventures, and they both agreed that he had had a most exciting day.

It will soon be time for Winkle-Pip to walk out into our world again – so be careful if you meet him, and do try to use your wish in the best way you can.